Echoes of
Thunder

Echoes of Thunder

Volume III of the Livingstone Library

Shari Popejoy

Injoy, Inc.

Echoes of Thunder

Published by Injoy, Inc.
www.injoyinc.com
ISBN: 978-0-9794842-4-7

Cover design by Laurel Popejoy of Pure Image Photography and Graphics, www.pureimage@moogo.com.

Dedicated to

Richard C. Patton and his

legacy

He was a man whose clear blue eyes, tall proud stance, straight gaze and square shoulders, exuded a sense of confidence and integrity that still inspire a sense of awe in me today, over twenty-five years after his death. Wife to Rose, father of thirteen, grandfather of over sixty, and patriarch of a family of decent, honorable, good citizens, he left an inheritance to his children's children.

Table of Contents

Chapter 1 Joe and Ben Enter Stage Right

As a cloudy sky enfolds the midnight darkness until a lightening bolt reveals a hidden landscape, the shadows of the night hide a world that is vibrant, colorful and interesting. Just because you can't see the colors doesn't mean they are not there, hidden and asleep. Just because someone's eyes are closed doesn't mean they are dead, and just because you haven't seen all of the Livingstones' world doesn't mean that it isn't there; part of the Livingstone world has only been glimpsed in flashes of lightening.

Likewise, just because someone's story has not yet been told, does not mean they have no role in an important and meaningful production. As living characters, we are no mere actors, making a brief appearance as an extra, and then dismissed until we are rewritten into the script in some future episode. No, our lives have purpose and destiny even when we are not center stage.

In a script, the playwright can write in bit parts and extras, whose main role is to support the main characters. When their role ends, their character ends, and no one really misses them, but not so in real life. Even when a character is not on center stage, their story continues in a real and important way. Even while they are hiding behind the curtains their role affects the performance.

When the Livingstone family arrived at Rhemawood, four of the children quickly became the main characters as their drama unfolded in a story that is told in a book entitled *Speak No Evil*. They returned to the stage in their roles as another character took center stage when the curtain opened on Tina's dramatic story, written down in a book called *Song of Rebellion*. That drama ended as the last act closed with a climactic sforzando of the orchestra that continues to echo in this story.

However, some important characters have been waiting behind the scenes to make their grand entrance, and their debut is imminent. And, now I must fade out on the Livingstone quartet for a time, while I set the stage for the next act. Rest assured, they will make their entrance in a later scene right on cue, and you will see how it all plays out as the curtain opens on a new scene. So, dim the lights, open the curtain, and enjoy the show.

Joe crammed his duffel bag with the last item it would swallow, pulled the drawstring, looked around at the pile of stuff on his dorm bed, and said, "All right, Ben, can you fit any of this in your suitcase?"

Ben looked dubiously at his carefully folded clothes arranged neatly in his suitcase. "I don't think it will Joe, but maybe I could leave something behind," he said in consternation, as he hesitantly surveyed Joe's stack.

"Oh, never mind. It would take you twenty minutes to decide and repack. I'll just wear it," he said. He picked up a pair of jeans and slipped them right over his shorts. He shrugged on the suit coat, rolled up the sleeves a couple turns, which made it look creatively casual with his black t-shirt. He pulled out some thick leather sandals from his bag, replacing them with his thinner flip-flops, flung his camera around his neck, squashed the case flat, placing it where the sandals had been, and finally flung a scarf around his neck, and placed the hat on his head. As he flung the pack over his shoulder, he said, "Come on, Ben. The shuttle is waiting to take us to the airport."

Ben shook his head and thought, "How can Joe look at a pile of mismatched items, and turn them into a cool outfit, and actually look better than he did before?" He pushed his glasses up on his nose, zipped his suitcase, and plopped his baseball cap on his head.

Joe took a quick look around the dorm room, and headed out the door. Ben scrambled to pick up his suitcase, grab the laptop, switch off the lights, and with a quick look around the deserted room, pulled the door shut and scrambled down the hall after Joe.

As they passed a group of students in the hall, several fond farewells were called after them.

"Take it easy Joe."

"Don't work too hard Joe."

"Hey, Joe, don't forget to email me those instructions."

Joe held up his hand in a farewell gesture as he headed down the stairs, and as the door swung shut someone called, "Bye Ben."

"What instructions?" Ben asked curiously, as he balanced his luggage, and tried to catch up with Joe.

"Oh, he thinks I'm going to send him the recipe for my Flying Flambé," said Joe.

"You're not, are you?" Ben gasped.

"Of course not. That recipe is going to win me first prize in the national festival this year," scoffed Joe. "He's crazy if he thinks I'd send it to him."

"Well did you tell him you would? He seemed pretty confidant," Ben said.

"No way," said Joe. "He's been wheedling all term. Started off saying, 'I wish I had the recipe,' then moved on to 'Wouldn't it be great to work together on it?' then began to say 'When I get that recipe,' and finally just started talking like it was a done deal. I never even answered him, and now just because he says it's so, he thinks it's so. His assumption is based on fantasy and not fact, and if he'd been quiet long enough for my reply, he would have heard my no."

"Oh, good," Ben said in relief.

"Had you worried again?" asked Joe with a grin. "You need to relax, Ben. You'll have more fun if you can learn to not take everything so seriously."

"Well, I try, but I feel like I have to keep an eye on you," said Ben with concern.

"Old Gentleman Ben," said Joe with a laugh. "Loosen up, and have some fun."

Ben shuffled the suitcase and laptop as he hurried after Joe trying to think back and remember if he'd packed everything. As they went through the lobby, Ben noticed two men who stood talking. One of them nodded toward Joe and said something in a low voice to the other man, who turned and looked at Joe with eyebrows raised.

"Joe, do you have a minute?" asked the first man.

"Sure Mr. Morris," Joe answered, as Ben looked with concern at the loaded shuttle in the circle drive outside the dorm, waiting to transport them to the airport.

"This is Tom Jacobson of Colossal Creations. I've been

telling him of your experiments."

"Oh, hello, Mr. Jacobson. It's good to meet you." Joe reached out and shook Mr. Jacobson's hand firmly and confidently. Mr. Jacobson seemed surprised to be met with such courtesy and confidence from a teenager.

Mr. Jacobson answered smoothly, as one accustomed to sizing up an opponent and taking the assertive role. "Dave here tells me that you have an interesting new concoction that will be a big hit."

"Yes. Mr. Morris has seen it in all its glory," Joe said with a pleased grin.

"Well, I'd like to buy it, my boy. I'll pay a good price for it," said Mr. Jacobson with a gleam in his eye.

"That's a great compliment, but I have plans of my own for it," Joe said decidedly. 'I plan to win the national festival."

"I can write you a check right now," said Mr. Jacobson drawing an expensive leather wallet from the breast pocket of his suit coat. "It'll buy you a lot of electronic gadgets or a car," said Mr. Jacobson temptingly.

Joe hesitated a second in surprise at the offer. "That's very generous of you, Mr. Jacobson, but I really don't have time to adequately consider your proposal right now."

"And it wouldn't be fair to keep the shuttle waiting any longer," said Ben pulling Joe toward the glass doors.

"This is a solid offer, and a guaranteed return on your efforts, young man," called Mr. Jacobson in a lecturing tone. "It's the difference between winning at the festival and winning the lottery. Besides, there's no guarantee that your plans will succeed."

"And no indication that they'll fail," said Joe with a grin. "But, thank you for your interest. It was nice meeting you, Mr. Jacobson. Good-bye, Mr. Morris. Thank you for all your advice this semester," Joe called over his shoulder as Ben pulled him to the shuttle.

"You bet," said Mr. Morris. "Good luck, Joe, and you too, Ben." He turned to Mr. Jacobson. "I told you it was no use. That boy has big plans for his future, and he won't make any decisions without his parents' approval anyway."

"We'll see about that," said Mr. Jacobson looking after Joe with a greedy gleam in his eye.

As Joe and Ben hustled through the airport checkpoints and settled into their seats with barely a moment to spare, Ben said, "Was that Mr. Jacobson serious?"

"Yeah, I think so," said Joe. "You know I've been telling you this would be a big hit."

"Yes, but enough to buy a car?" asked Ben. "That's a lot of money."

"It sure is, and even more if we play our cards right. If he's willing to pay that much for it, think how much it's really worth," Joe contemplated.

"Yeah. I guess so," said Ben.

"Just stick to the plan, Benny Boy, and it will be spectacular," said Joe with a dramatic gesture of his hands, like an explosion of brilliance.

After a quiet pause Ben spoke again. "Do you think Mom's been missing us?" he asked with an eager look out the airplane window.

"Not as much as you've been missing her," said Joe with a chuckle. "This is the longest you've been away from home, isn't it?"

"Well not the longest away from home of course, but the longest away from family," said Ben.

"Hey, what am I?" asked Joe with an elbow jab at his younger brother.

"You know what I mean," said Ben. "It will be good to get home again."

"Well, technically we're not going home. We're headed to Rhemawood, but I guess home is where the family is -- wherever that happens to be this month," Joe grinned.

"So what exactly is Rhemawood?" asked Ben.

"Don't you remember anything about Rhemawood? We were there about ten years ago when we were kids," explained Joe.

"I just can't remember what it was like," said Ben.

"Well, it's like a castle, and there are tunnels, and this huge library where I used to do my homework, and a mountain, and trails, and woods and a lake."

"Sounds great," said Ben, "Bet the kids are loving it," he said with a grin.

"Yeah, if I know them, they've already discovered all the great places, but I bet there's one thing they haven't found," he said with a chuckle.

"What is it?" asked Ben eagerly.

"Well, there's this cave on the mountain, and a secret entrance I found, and I hid a treasure in the cave. It's in an old metal lunchbox filled with all my best things. I wonder if it is still there," Joe said mysteriously.

"Will you be able to find it again?" asked Ben.

"Of course – with my sense of direction, I should be able to go right to it. Besides I left some clues and marks along the way."

"Well, they better not be too obvious or Luke would have discovered it by now," Ben said, and Joe chuckled in agreement.

"Hey, why don't I remember?" asked Ben "Where was I when you were having all those great adventures?"

"You still had to take naps back then," said Joe.

"And Mom just let you explore in caves while I was napping?" Ben asked suspiciously.

"Well, I was supposed to be doing schoolwork in the abbey library, but I found a secret tunnel behind one of the bookshelves that led to this cave. Sometimes I would just happen to be looking for a book, and the door would accidentally swing open, and I just sorta kinda wandered into the cave – looking for the answers to my homework, you know."

"Yeah, right," Ben grinned. "Sounds like you were doing research, for a science project or something.

"Well, Mom never told me I couldn't wander into the cave, and bury a treasure," said Joe defensively, "And as long as I got my schoolwork finished, she never suspected a thing. It turned out to be a great motivator, and I'm sure she would have been very grateful for the help – you were such a handful, you know," Joe joked.

"Ha," said Ben. "We both know Mom loves me best," he teased.

"Yeah, because you're such a good wittle boy," said Joe mockingly as he jerked Ben's ball cap sideways on his head.

"No. I just know how to make her happy," said Ben with a grin. "I don't do anything that would rock the boat," Ben said as he slid down in his seat for a nap.

"Or the cradle. You've been that way since you were born. The perfect child," Joe rolled his eyes.

"Well, I just watched you make all the mistakes, and learned what not to do. Thank you very much, by the way. You saved me a lot of trouble," said Ben, turning toward the window as he settled in for a nap.

"I think I got into enough trouble for both of us," laughed

Joe. "Glad those days are over."

"Maybe you've learned a thing or two from me, too," said Ben. "Now you're the perfect child," Ben said as he began to doze off.

"Well, perfectly talented, and perfectly creative, and perfectly successful, and perfectly --" Joe continued his list, as Ben added sleepily, "Humble."

Chapter 2   Lights, Action, Camera!

As the last movement of the symphony began, Luke knelt down and set Tina Turtle on the ground. He closed his eyes and listened to the perfect blending of the music as it began the final crescendo. Just as it reached the climax of the music, as the brass blared, the woodwinds sustained, and the timpani proclaimed, there was a huge explosion on the mountaintop, and a boulder catapulted down the mountainside amidst a cloud of smoke and flashing explosions.

The disciplined orchestra continued to follow the direction of the conductor. Luke looked in surprise up the mountainside to the clearing smoke, and then over to his dad, who silently nodded to the conductor to signal him to continue. He spoke into his headset to signal the cameraman to zoom in on the action created on the mountainside as the boulder continued to catapult to the bottom of the gorge.

As the smoke cleared Luke saw a movement behind one of the boulders on the mountaintop, and crept closer to one of the cameras. He picked up a lens and twisted it to zoom up on the boulder. He chuckled silently as he observed the jaunty hat poking over the boulder as the perpetrator surveyed the scene he had created.

As the last notes of the sustained played, Luke waited for the conductor's cut off, and as soon as the director yelled "Cut!" he raced up the mountainside, grabbed the cap, shoved it on his own head, and cried, "When did you get here, Joe?"

"Long enough to perfect this scene for Dad. Wasn't that a great effect?"

"It sure was," Luke agreed. "Right on tempo, at just the right moment in the musical score" Luke said with admiration, and looking around added, "Hey, where's Ben?"

"Oh, he couldn't wait to see Mom, so he headed to the Rookery, but I didn't want to miss the opportunity to make a grand entrance," Joe said. "Hey, Dad, did you get that recorded?" Joe called to his father, who was coming up the hillside to greet him, after giving some directions to the camera crew.

Dad gave Joe a big bear hug and said, "We'll talk about that later."

"Yeah. Wasn't it great?" said Joe with delight. "Just like I planned. It couldn't have been more perfect."

"Unless you'd maybe cleared it with the director?" suggested Dad.

"There wasn't time for that, and we would have missed the perfect lighting, if we'd had to wait for another take after lunch. You have to admit that," Joe said cockily.

Dad nodded, "You're right – it worked out this time, but you can't take success for granted. You never know when the variables will turn away from your favor."

"Never," Joe boasted. "I have been blessed with favor," he said proudly.

Dad looked at him with concern as he added quietly, "Take heed lest you fall."

But Joe didn't hear the old proverb as he turned to greet Logan and Rachael, and answer Dori's squeal of delight as she ran to jump in her older brother's arms.

"Joey, you're back. I missed you so much," said Dori, hugging him tightly.

Joe struggled to loosen her tiny choking arms from his neck, "You mithed me tho muth?" he teased. "What happened to your teeth?" he asked laughing as he looked at the gap in her mouth where her teeth used to be.

"They fell out, and then we came to Rhemawood, and met Miss Sophia, and then Tina came and she got losted in the cave, and we heard music playing, and we didn't know it was Dad's orchestra, and did you hear the explosion and see the giant rock?"

Joe laughed, "TMI. I can't hear all about six weeks of activity in six seconds," he said as he jostled her to his back, gave Rachael a one-armed hug, and took his hat off Luke's head and plopped it on Logan's.

"Joe, why don't you go with the kids and say hello to your mother. I have some things to finish up here. Tell her I'll come home for lunch, and we can all sit down together around the table and catch up. It's good to have you home, son."

They took off up the mountainside chatting gaily, Dori still on Joe's back.

"So Joe, how did you manage to get that boulder to

go the right direction at just the right moment?" Luke asked, his head down studying his GPS as he led them to the best route back home to the rookery.

After a moment of silence, Luke raised his head, looked over his shoulder, and stopped in amazement. If noise is amplified it becomes deafening. Likewise silence amplified is deafening. He was standing alone on the hillside. Everyone had disappeared. The silent stillness was broken by a ripple of Dori's giggling. He pushed a bush aside and saw Dori standing alone beside a large boulder.

"Where are the others?" he asked in surprise.

Dori just shrugged her shoulders with a mischievous grin. Luke looked around, up and down, and finally discovered a hidden opening in the ground behind the boulder. It looked like a small den in the ground, but in the underground darkness he noticed flat rocks like a stairway leading down. As he descended into the ground, Logan flipped on his flashlight, and Rachael and Joe laughed at his surprise.

"How'd you find this so fast?" Luke asked.

"Oh, I know a lot of secrets of Rhemawood," Joe said mysteriously. "Follow me."

They followed him through the cave, and soon the walls changed, from damp rough cave walls to hewn stone. They were in the tunnel system that traversed the hillside of Rhemawood, but this was a different tunnel than the ones they had explored. They passed stairs and corridors, but Joe didn't stop until he came to a final stairway. "Do you know what is at the top of these stairs?" he asked.

Luke studied his GPS said, "We're almost back home, according to the coordinates of my GPS, but this isn't the tunnel that leads to the cellar of the rookery."

"Go up and see," said Joe with a grin. Luke took the flashlight Logan offered and went up the stairs. At the top a large rock wall blocked his way. Logan, following close behind said, "Who would make a stairway to a rock wall?"

"Precisely," said Luke, feeling around for a latch or hidden door. He pushed on a rock that stuck out from the rest, and suddenly the wall swung out just enough to let him pass through, and when he walked through the opening, he was in the backyard of the rookery. From the yard, this appeared to be a large boulder on the mountainside that, with the other boulders, formed a natural enclosure to one side of the yard. Brick walls enclosed the rest of the yard, and one wall of the yard included the garden door that opened up to the trail that led to Miss Sophia's tower.

"Come on, Joey. Mom can't wait to see you," Dori said as she took his hand and dragged him across the yard.

Rachael followed, eager to see the delight she knew would light up her mother's face when she saw her oldest son returned home after his long absence.

Luke stayed to find the lever that returned the boulder to its original place. He wanted to continue searching for other hidden tunnels, behind all the big boulders, but Logan called, "Come on, let's go see Ben," and the two raced across the yard into the back door of the house. They ran through the door just in time to hear Joe say, "Oh, by the way, Dad says he's coming home for lunch."

Mom had both hands clasped around Joe's left hand, but she dropped his hand, which Dori grabbed, while Mom went into action like a well-trained colonel marshaling the troops.

"Ben, will you get the grill going?" she asked sweetly.

"Hey, flames are my specialty," said Joe, untangling himself from Dori, and heading out the door to check on the grill and get it heating, while Ben grabbed the tongs, platter, hot pads, and everything else that Joe would be asking for in about two minutes.

"Boys, will you chop up these vegetables and get

them ready to go on the grill as soon as it's hot?" she said to Luke and Logan as she nodded to a mound of colorful vegetables on the island countertop.

"Sure," said Logan as he grabbed a knife, and Luke grabbed a cutting board.

"Rachael, would you turn this fruit into some sort of salad? And Dori, would you set the table for us?"

Mom surveyed her productive crew with a contented smile. It was good to have them all together again.

By the time Dad arrived, Dori had set the patio table with a pretty cloth, real plates in honor of the return of Joe and Ben, and had iced glasses ready for the pitcher filled with lemonade tinkling with ice cubes and lemon wedges.

The vegetables were pulled steaming from the grill, Rachael's fruit salad added color to the table, and the meat was ready to be grilled to last-minute perfection by Dad.

Mom had just pulled a pan of fluffy rolls from the oven, and Ben eyed them hungrily as he leaned over the pan and breathed deeply. "I actually dreamed about your rolls last night, Mom," Ben said as he straightened up and kissed Mom on the cheek. She smiled as she kissed him back and said, "It is so good to have you home, son."

"And you, too," she said as she wrapped her arms around Joe and hugged him from the side as he stood at the grill watching Dad. "I think you've grown again," she said fondly, looking up at him.

"Grown in good looks and charm," he said as he turned and gave her a quick peck on the cheek.

As Dad brought the steaks from the grill, they settled down at the deck table, grateful to be together again. Joe and Ben took turns telling about their term at school, and Luke, Logan, Rachael and Dori supplied them with info about their adventures at Rhemawood.

"It's so good to have my young men back home again," said Mom as she looked from Joe to Ben. She had a look of pride in her eye when she glanced at Joe, which softened to a tender look of adoration when she looked at Ben.

It takes a lifetime to learn about the many sides of love, and sometimes families get distracted by the facets of love, and don't enjoy the true brilliance of the gem. As a diamond turns and catches the light, it reveals different glory from different angles. The love a little girl has for her daddy is adorable, but is subtly different from the love a grown woman feels for her aging father as she sees his body weakened with wear, his spirit strengthened with sage.

The hugs and kisses and confidant squeals of a girl tossed in the air by a vibrant strong father, knowing he will always catch her, provide a special feeling of security. But it is of no less value than silently watching the dwindling sun setting in a rosy sky with golden-lined clouds, with her father's gnarled hand placed on her own mature one many years later.

In the same way, the pride and delight that pours over a mother while witnessing one child's accomplishments is not superior to the feeling of love and delight she feels when a different child climbs into her lap and covers her in hugs and kisses. The facets of a diamond all combine to produce its brilliance.

In a similar way, shared joys can be equal to shared sorrows. Shared accomplishments can be equal to shared disappointments. The feeling is not equal (no one can say a sunburn is equal to dessert), but the result can be equal. A person with a painful sunburn might welcome a soothing ointment with more joy than they would covet a piece of chocolate cake. Sharing a difficult moment with humanity can make it more meaningful, as a family can readily tell you.

So, how can a woman with as many children as this mother had, love them all equally? Well, she can't, and she doesn't love them equally, but a healthy mother loves each child completely. That love is shown differently to each child, and if each child will accept that love in their own special way, then they have a treasure that belongs to them alone, not to be divided or competed for, but to be accepted and honored, as the true gift of mothers.

And when you add the mother love to the father love, and the parent-child love, and brother-sister, brother-brother, sister-sister love that was in evidence around this table, it represented a lot of love. This love was shown by good-natured teasing, compliments, hugs, elbow jabs, and hair rumpling, or maybe just a grin or look across the table, or the tone of voice. So, as the mother enjoyed having her children back together around the table, they all enjoyed the reunion and all tried to talk at once.

"Yeah, and you're just in time for the picnic tonight," said Logan.

"Yeah," said Rachael. "It's the traditional production kick-off, and we're having an old-fashion barn dance –"

"With live music," said Luke.

"And Barbie-cue, and baked beans, and corn on the cob," said Dori excitedly.

"Which you won't be able to eat," teased Joe.

Dori's mouth dropped in sudden disappointment, but she grinned, showing the huge gap where her front teeth were missing, when Ben leaned over and whispered to her, "Don't worry, I'll cut it off the cob for you with my pocket knife. I have a special blade for that," he winked.

"Are we having fireworks?" added Joe.

"Well, I hadn't really planned anything, but if you would like to arrange something, you can," Dad answered.

"Are you kidding? Show me your armory, and I'll put together the best display you have ever seen," said Joe confidently.

"As long as you abide by the first rule," said Dad.

"I know, I know," said Joe, rolling his eyes.

"Safety first," shouted all the children in unison.

"Wait until you see the Flying Flambé," said Joe proudly. "I finally got it perfected. Mr. Morris said he thinks it will win a prize at the national festival."

"Someone wanted to buy it," said Ben, passing the vegetables to Rachael.

"Really?" Dad asked with interest.

"Oh, yeah – just Mr. Jacobson of Colossal Creations," said Joe with feigned modesty.

"Did he actually make you an offer?" Dad asked.

"Well he never actually quoted a figure, but he pulled out his wallet," said Joe.

"And he said Joe could buy a car with the earnings," Ben said.

"You're kidding," said Dad. "He thought you would sell it without the advice of your parents?"

"Well, it is my design," Joe persisted arrogantly.

"Of course it is, but honorable people don't try to do business with a minor," Dad explained. "Even adults would have paperwork with a business sale like that. I'm glad you weren't swayed by his offer. I'm proud of you for using your head."

"Well, if the offer had been good enough, I might have taken him up on it," said Joe, "but this design is gonna make me rich and famous."

"Joe, there's more to being successful in business than just designing a product. You have to market and sell it after you design it. Sometimes it makes good sense to sell your design to another company, and sometimes it makes better sense to work the plan yourself, but that's where good advice and counsel and wisdom come in," Dad explained patiently, "So even though it might make good business sense to sell it, I don't think it's wise to do business with a man who tried to buy your design without giving you time to consider the proposal or get advice from your parents.

As they talked business, Dori said, "Mom, you should have heard Tina play her violin today. It was beautiful," she sighed.

"I know. I've heard her play before. She is a talented girl," Mom agreed.

"Talent wouldn't have been enough though, because she almost decided not to play today," said Dori.

"Well, that choice would have made it sad for Dori, but there was another violinist ready to play the part if she hadn't arrived," said Mom.

"Someone is always waiting to seize the opportunity," Dad said wisely.

"Well, just let someone try to seize my glory," said Joe, "I won't share it with them," he laughed, but Luke saw Mom and Dad glance at each other, and he knew they were talking without saying a word, as they often did.

When the family finished the meal, they all rose and grabbed plates and utensils and serving dishes, and soon had the patio straightened. Mom and the girls offered to do the dishes, as Dad headed back to work, and the guys went to settle in.

"Well, Luke, I guess we'll be bunking together as usual?" Joe asked.

"Unless you want to bunk with Ben and me," said Logan. "Wait until you see the cool three-level bunks in our room."

"Yeah. There's a fireman's pole, too," said Ben as he raced Logan to the second story, where there ensued a loud and lively unpacking and settling in by the four brothers.

Chapter 3 Grab Your Pardner

Rachael hoisted a hay bale on top of another, climbed up, took the hammer and nail Dori handed her, and with a few well-aimed strokes hammered the nail into the floor joists of the barn loft, and hooked the metal handle of the lantern over the nail. She hopped down and surveyed their work. "Dori, those lanterns will look great when they're lit."

"Yes, but where will we put the refreshments?" Dori asked.

"Well, we could have tables brought over from the dining hall of the mansion, but I think it would look too fancy. Let's look around and see if we can come up with another idea."

"What about these old doors?" Dori pointed to several oak doors stacked in an empty stall.

"They're perfect, Dori. We can stack a couple hay bales together and set the door across them. Help me," Rachael said excitedly.

After they swept the old hay from the concrete floor, put some hay bales across one end of the barn for the musicians, and used a stack of bandannas Mom had sent to add some color, the girls stepped back to admire their work.

"Oh, I almost forgot this basket of gourds mom sent. We can turn these into decorations for the refreshment table," Rachael said.

"And look at this, Rachael. We could use this to put ice and drinks in," Dori said as she pulled a galvanized tub from the tool room."

"Hey, what else is in there?" Rachael asked. She pulled open the door and excitedly grabbed old farm tools, handing them to Dori, and saying, "Find a nail and hang these up. They make great decorations. Old cross saws and shovels and saw blades, and halters and bridles, and things they didn't know the names of, became decorations for the walls of the barn.

If Dori couldn't find a nail, Rachael pounded one in the wall, and soon the stable walls were covered with antique treasures that created a perfect setting for the barn dance.

"Cone on Dori, I think we're finished here. We better go get dressed. What are you going to wear?"

"I'm going to wear my overalls. Will you braid my hair?"

✗

When they arrived at the section of the abbey where the

fireworks were stored, they found boxes of explosives stacked on pallets. A man with a two-day growth of red and gray whiskers sat on a chair with his feet on a paper-strewn desk. When he saw them, he hastily dropped his legs from the desk, grabbed a clipboard and a pencil, and busily began to make marks on the top paper, eying the boys warily.

Joe strode forward and stuck his hand out confidently, "I'm Joe Livingstone," The man stuck his pencil behind his ear, wiped his hand on his jeans a couple times, and hesitantly shook Joe's hand as he said, "I'm Jake – uh -- Ubsen."

"It's good to meet you Mr. Ubsen. Dad said we'd find you here," Joe said.

"Oh, just call me Jake," he chuckled nervously, then cleared his throat and said in a louder tone that seemed a bit accusing. "So, you know about peerotechnics?" he said, eying Joe out of the corner of his eye.

"Yes. I've been working with them for a few years. We're going to put together a display for tonight," Joe responded.

"Oh," he said, "Well just help yourself," he said pointing to a pallet of prepackaged Roman candles.

"Well, I'm actually going to need several ingredients, so if you'll give me a pick ticket, I'll write it up as we go along," Joe explained.

"Oh, you don't need to bother with that. Just take what you need," said Mr. Ubsen.

Joe looked at him in surprise, "We'll need to keep track of the inventory, and give an account at the end of the production for all of the explosives that are used, so if you just give me the form –"

Mr. Ubsen looked surprised, and slightly irritated as he shuffled through some papers on a cluttered desk.

"Here's one," said Ben, pulling a two-page carbonless form from under a stack, handing it directly to Joe.

"So, what do you have in mind for tonight, Joe?" Luke asked.

"Well, I'll use some prepackaged fireworks, but we're going to put together some of our own special ones," Joe said with excitement.

Mr. Ubsen looked at them as though they were kindergärtners who had just told him they were going to take the jeep out for a spin.

"Luke, see if you can find the Potassium Nitrate," Joe said.

"Don't have none," Mr. Ubsen said from where he had sat down on a crate.

Joe looked at him in surprise, "You don't have Potassium Nitrate?"

"Nope," Mr. Ubsen said.

"That's one of the main ingredients in pyrotechnics," Joe said in disbelief.

"Most of the new guys are using Sodium Nitrite these days," Mr. Ubsen said as though Joe didn't know the latest info.

"Is that so?" Joe asked, looking at him warily.

"Yeah," Mr. Ubsen said, shifting his weight.

"Well, I'll be needing some Potassium Nitrate. How soon can you get a delivery?"

"Probably not for a week or two," Mr. Ubsen said.

"Well, place an order and go ahead and expedite the shipping so we can get it sooner," Joe said authoritatively.

"That'll cost extra," Mr. Ubsen lectured.

"I know, but it can't be helped. We need Potassium Nitrate."

"It'll have to be approved by Mr. Livingstone," Mr. Ubsen argued.

Ben handed Joe a piece of paper with 'Supply Requisition' written across the top. He had already filled in the item number, quantity and supplier, and it was ready for Joe's signature. Joe initialed the form, handed it to Mr. Ubsen and said with confidence, "He'll approve it."

Mr. Ubsen just harrumphed, but took the paper.

"Luke, just get a box of Sodium nitrate, and meet me in the lab," Joe said.

"You mean Sodium nitrite?" Logan asked.

"No," Joe said with a significant glance at Mr. Ubsen, "Sodium nitrate with an a."

Joe told the boys what he needed, Ben called out the item number, Luke found the crate, and Logan entered it on the pick list.

"Get some bentonite," Joe said.

"Don't' have none," said Mr. Ubsen.

Joe just shook his head in disbelief and said to Luke, "Can you run to the rookery and get some kitty litter?"

"Sure," Luke answered, and without asking why, ran out the door to do Joe's bidding.

"Add that to the requisition," Joe told Ben.

Mr. Ubsen alternated between tucking in his shirttail, and pulling his pants up by the belt loops as he followed Joe around. Ben busied himself with straightening up the forms and paperwork on the desk. When they had all the supplies they needed, they headed to the combination lab/workshop that Joe had set up in one of the empty classrooms of the abbey.

"So, what's the difference with Sodium Nitrite and Sodium Nitrate?" Logan asked as he hurried to catch up with Joe and Ben.

"Sodium Nitrite is used as a food preservative. Sodium Nitrate is used in explosives. They have a similar chemical make-up, and are both considered salts, but they have very different uses.

"Yeah, don't shake Sodium Nitrate on your food, or you'll be in for a bang," Logan laughed.

"So why did you want Potassium Nitrate instead of Sodium Nitrate?" Luke asked as he came into the lab with a bag of kitty litter over his shoulder.

"Are you familiar with the flame test?" Joe asked.

"Yeah, a little. Isn't that the color flame that a chemical produces when burned?" Luke answered.

"Sure is. Every element produces a unique flame. Sodium burns yellow, calcium burns orange, and arsenic burns blue. And in pyrotechnics, it is very important because the materials you use in the rocket affect the color of the explosives and the beauty of the display," Joe said as he opened his toolbox and arranged his tools neatly on the workbench.

"Okay, Logan, you get out ten cardboard tubes, and set them up in this rack," Joe instructed. "We're going to make some rockets!"

"Ben, you show Luke how to make a nozzle on the end.

"So what's the kitty litter for?" Logan asked.

"Well, kitty litter is mostly bentonite clay, and it hardens into a nice nozzle for the exhaust end of the casing. It allows the gasses to build up more pressure, which increases the exhaust velocity, or thrust, which propels the rocket into the sky. But, we have to make the exhaust hole the proper size, because the higher pressure, also makes it burn faster, and if it burns too fast, then the casing explodes before it has a chance to make it into the air, and we have a CATO," Joe explained.

"What's a CATO?" Logan asked.

"Catastrophe at take off," Joe said.

"Like a dud?" Logan asked.

"Could be. Or it could be a potentially unpredictable and dangerous explosion," Joe said. "So, let's quit talking and get to work. We don't have too much time before the dance."

Joe showed them how to fill the paper tube with gun powder and stars, and how to insert the black match wick, and showed them a few tricks of taping the wick to delay the blast, and attaching and balancing the rod that would hold the rocket in the ground at the right angle for the proper trajectory for the display.

"Joe, will you double check these nozzles to make sure the exhaust hole isn't too big?" Ben asked.

"Sure. I'll do that as soon as I show Logan how to cut these fuses. This wick is filled with gunpowder, so cut a ten-inch section, but cut it at a forty-five degree angle so more of the gunpowder is exposed. If you just make a straight cut, just a small round center section of gunpowder is exposed, but if you cut it at an angle, then a lot more is exposed. See?" Joe said, demonstrating it for Logan.

"Wow. That does show a lot more gun powder," Logan exclaimed.

"Yeah. Pays to remember your angles from geometry," Joe grinned.

They built several types of rockets and shells, and when they had them built, they headed to the barn to set up.

Joe took the lead in setting up the display. Mr. Ubsen tried to help. He wasn't sure that Joe really knew what he was doing, and tried to give him advice, but Joe just continued to set up what he assured them would be a spectacular display.

Then they all headed back to the rookery to get dressed for the barn dance.

Dori wore a comfy pair of faded overalls that were suddenly too short, so Rachael helped her roll up the pant legs. With her rolled up overalls, red braids, and missing front teeth, she looked like a country girl ready to go to a barn dance.

Rachael decided to wear a cute denim skirt that flared at the bottom, and as she swung Dori around, the skirt spread out in a circle around her. Luke, coming down the stairs said, "That skirt is really pretty, Rachael – perfect for dancing."

"Thanks, Luke. You always know how to make a girl feel good," Rachael said with a pleased smile.

Logan raced past Rachael on the stairs without taking time to admire her skirt, and shouted as he looked out the window, "Oh, wow! Look what Dad is driving."

The four ran to the door, just as Dad set the brake and jumped down from a horse-drawn wagon, piled high with hay bales.

"Oh, the horses are so pretty," squealed Dori as she ran out the door. "Can I pet them, Daddy?"

"Sure. Just make sure to stay in the front of them where they can see you, and don't get in between the wagon and the horses," he cautioned.

"Can I drive them, Dad?" Logan begged.

"Well, if Mom doesn't mind sitting in back, you can drive until we pick up the other children at the mansion," Dad said.

"Oh, I don't mind," said Mom as she took Luke's hand, climbed nimbly into the back of the wagon, and sat down on a hay bale next to Dori. After they all climbed aboard, Dad gave Logan a lesson on how to drive a team of horses. Luke stood in the wagon, behind Logan, paying close attention to the way Dad held the reigns, and released the brake, and talked to the team. Luke examined the harnesses and the reigns, and how they connected to the horses. He was figuring it all out so that when he got a chance to drive the team, he would be ready.

Logan dropped one of the reigns, and in his attempt to bend over and pick it up, he accidentally touched the horse with the whip. Then while he apologized to the horse, he started to veer off the side of the road, as he gave a wrong signal to the horse with the reigns. Dad patiently reached over and readjusted the reins in Logan's hands, grinning at his attempt to apologize to the horse.

"Pull in here, Son," Dad said, nodding to the mansion, a large three-story home turned hotel, where some of the crew and their families were staying during the production. As they drove up to the mansion, more families were boarding a hay wagon pulled behind an old green tractor. Many of the children wanted to ride the horse drawn wagon, so the Livingstones made way for them and welcomed them aboard.

It was a merry party that made their way to the barn, and by the time they had gone around the mountainside on an old-fashion hayride, it was dusk when they arrived at the barn. They enjoyed a meal around an old chuck wagon and campfire, and soon the lanterns were lit, and the musicians tuned up their instruments.

Dori said, "Oh, look, Tina's Dad is playing a violin,"

"That's not a violin, Dori. That's a fiddle," Luke corrected.

"What's the difference?" Dori asked.

"It's all in the toes," said Logan with a grin. Dori gave him a puzzled look.

"You'll hear the difference as soon as they start playing," Rachael explained.

Just then Tina's Dad said, "1, 2, 3, 4," and the small group of musicians took off on an upbeat, toe-tapping, foot stomping song to welcome the dancers, and the party was off and running.

"Hey, Rache—wanna dance?" Logan asked, and Rachael eagerly nodded as he took her hand, and whisked her to the dance floor.

Luke looked around and saw Tina standing shyly over by the musicians, holding her pink violin case. He walked over to her and said kindly, "Are you playing music tonight?"

"I don't' know. I guess," she said slowly, looking longingly at the dancers lining up for a Virginia Reel.

"You really played well today," he said with admiration.

"Thank you," she said shyly.

"You know, I think you've played enough for one day. Would you like to dance instead?"

"I don't know how to dance like that," she said lowering her voice. Tina wasn't used to admitting that she didn't know everything.

"Oh, it is really easy. They call out the steps, and tell you what to do next. I'll help you if you want to learn," he said.

"Well, I guess I could try," she said slowly, "but I don't like to make mistakes."

"Oh, in these dances, even if you run into someone or step on their toes, if you just laugh and smile, and say 'excuse me', they won't mind – they probably won't even notice," he said with a grin.

He offered his hand, and she hesitantly took it. He walked quickly, and soon they were running to the middle of the barn, and lined up with the rest of the dancers, as the caller shouted, "Bow to your partner."

Luke bowed, and Tina, following the cue of Rachael, made a lady-like courtesy.

She was dressed in a frilly pink dress, and her dark hair had been curled to perfection, and pulled back from her face with ribbons. Her blue eyes shone with delight as Luke nodded approval to her, as she do-si-do'd like the other girls. It was just a matter of following directions as the commands were shouted out. Right-hand swing, left-hand swing. Soon she was smiling with delight, and by the end of the dance, Luke had no trouble handing her off to one of the four boys who clamored for the next dance with her.

"That was very nice of you, Luke," Rachael said, but he didn't have time to reply, because he noticed Dori standing alone, while the disappointed, and undutiful boys stood looking dejectedly after Tina and her partner, leaving Dori unattended. He quickly walked over in front of the inattentive boys and said with a grand flourish as he made a gallant bow at the waist, almost touching the floor with his head, while saying in his best British accent, "May I have the pleasure of this dance?"

Dori giggled, showing her missing front teeth, as she said, "Sthure!"

Luke spent the first few dances making sure all the girls were having a good time, but when the music ended on the fourth dance, he wiped his brow and quietly headed out to check on Joe and the fireworks.

Joe had set up the fireworks command center at a safe distance from the barn. Mr. Ubsen was standing nearby with his hands in his pockets.

"Are you going to position those rockets?" he inquired questioningly.

"Yes, but not yet. I need to make sure they are in the right order first."

Mr. Ubsen grunted, but didn't argue. Instead, he turned to some displays and started to rearrange them. Joe noticed what he was doing and said, "We'll need to leave those there, Mr. Ubsen. I've placed them so that we'll get the exact trajectory we need."

Mr. Ubsen looked annoyed, but moved away from the fireworks.

Joe scurried around giving Ben directions, although Ben could practically read Joe's mind. He gave some direction to Mr. Ubsen, but Luke noticed that Joe had to redo the few instructions he'd given to Mr. Ubsen. Finally Joe just ignored him, and began to give instructions to Luke instead.

They worked busily while Mr. Ubsen lurked, trying to look busy, but it seemed that everything he touched, Joe had to reposition.

When it was dark enough, Joe set off his first explosion, which lit the night sky with brilliance. The music stopped, the dancers abandoned the dance floor, and the crowd gave an appropriate gasp of awe.

Joe was happy with the effect. He always liked to make a grand entrance, and this time he had even silenced the music. He saw Dad whisper to the conductor, who gave a command to the instrumentalists. After a brief shuffling of sheet music, they began to play the song to which Joe had choreographed the display.

The crescendos and drum cadences of this piece were a perfect accompaniment to the backdrop of the artistry in the night sky. However, Joe, never one to be content to be the background, took center stage and his pyrotechnic creations were worthy of the awe they inspired.

Using the night sky as a black canvas, Joe painted a brilliant masterpiece of colorful delights. The music from the ensemble provided a seamless intro to each explosion, and the perfect timing of the blasts provided a syncopation of rhythmic artistry. The perfect balance resulted in a symphony of color splashing across the sky. Although the conductor wove the music with his baton, it was Joe who was weaving a tapestry in the sky, entwined with music from the band.

As the piece gained intensity, so did the display, until in one climactic movement when the timpani were building the suspense, the crowd held their breath in hushed anticipation for the piece de résistance. Based on the preceding beauty, it would surely be magnificent, and as the conductor dramatically suspended the music, there was a whiz, a weak pop, and a shudder of smoke in the bushes near the open barn doors. Then flashes of explosions burst forth, as the guests shrieked and took cover from the exploding arsenal at the entrance of the barn.

Chapter 4   3-2-1 Blast Off

If a bolt of lightening had appeared from the sky and struck Joe, he could not have been more shocked. He was riveted in place as though frozen and electrified, while Ben rushed to survey the damage of the wayward rocket. Luke hurried to the barn to assure the guests that there was no danger, and slipped in just as Dad closed the sliding barn doors shut. Mom suggested it would be a good time for the guests to try the spiced cider. The moms counted their children, and made their way to the refreshment table, while Dad quietly went outside the barn to check on Joe. At Dad's stern, questioning look, Joe said with agitation, "Dad, I have no idea what happened." He replayed the setup in his mind.

"Maybe you didn't stabilize the rocket," said Dad. "I've told you many times that stabilization is one of the most important aspects of pulling off a successful display."

"No. I checked. I always check. You saw me check, didn't you, Ben?"

"I saw you stabilize it," agreed Ben.

"Yes, but did you double check it before the production?" Dad questioned.

"I always do," Joe replied.

"Yes, but did you this time?" Dad continued questioning.

Joe shrugged. "I don't think it was a stabilization problem."

"In this business that's not good enough," Dad declared. "You must always follow the same procedure."

Joe pursed his lips, and looked away, eager to end the lecture.

Dad put his hand on Joe's shoulder. "Joe, if I'm going to put you in charge of the pyrotechnics of this production, I have to know that I can count on you."

"You've always been able to count on me," Joe bristled, as he shrugged his Dad's hand from his shoulder – it felt like a weight of condemnation.

"I know, and we want to keep it that way. There is no room for pride or arrogance, or thinking that we're too perfect to make mistakes. That's why we follow set procedures, so we don't forget something. And we always double-check the stabilization," Dad said concluding his lecture.

Joe knew further defense was useless, so he nodded his head, and Dad patted his shoulder before turning to survey the damage. As Joe looked up he caught Ben's eye, who said comfortingly, "Don't worry Joe – everyone makes mistakes."

"Not me," said Joe. As he looked over Ben's shoulder, he saw Mr. Ubsen leaning against the barn with his arms folded, chewing on a hay stub.

It looked like the corner of his mouth was turned up in a grin, but when he caught Joe's eye, he said, "That's too bad. I woulda been glad to double-check that stabilization for you. Maybe next time I can be more help to you boys." He wandered off to get some cider while the boys made sure no embers remained outside the barn. Ben looked after Mr. Ubsen with concern. There was something about that man that made him uncomfortable.

Luke gave one last kick in the dirt to quench a final spark and headed into the barn with Joe. Miss Bottie, a jovial heavy-set woman was helping with refreshments, and handed Joe a cup of punch. She said, "I'm not sure that punch tastes right. I was making it when the explosion occurred and I lost count of how many cups of sugar I added."

"Well, it wasn't really an explosion," Joe explained, "Just a wayward rocket."

"Oh, my," she gasped. "Explosions are so dangerous. I always tell kids that they're going to blind themselves with their firecrackers, but boys will be boys."

Joe gave the talkative woman a puzzled look, as Luke hurried him away from the table and Miss Bottie's dire predictions.

They walked past a group of men and heard a familiar voice, "Yeah. You got to be careful with explosives. It's not a job for novices. In my thirty years in peerotechnics, I've learned to have a healthy respect for their power. It's like taming the lightening bolt."

Joe bristled and would have jumped into the conversation, but Luke said, "Hey, Joe, tell me about your Flying Flambé'"

Joe looked over his shoulder and caught Mr. Ubsen's contemptuous grin as he continued to explain his superior knowledge of peerotechnics to the other crewmembers.

"Tell you, I'll show you," Joe said. Luke followed him eagerly up a moonlit strewn path to the abbey. When they arrived Joe pulled out the normal ingredients used in fireworks, and explained how the configuration of explosives and delay created rockets.

"Every firework has the same key ingredients packed inside a cardboard tube: a visco fuse on the outside to ignite the lift charge to lift it into the air, with another slow burning fuse on the inside that explode the stars, which are chemicals that burn different colors. So, it's all about timing the lift, the explosion, and selecting the right ingredients and putting it together so it will be a beautiful display of color." Joe explained.

"So what makes the Flying Flambé' so special?" Luke asked.

"Well, every rocket has the same elements – light, color,

sound and of course lift. It is the combination of these that create a rocket. However – and here is the trick to the Flying Flambé' –"

Luke's eyes widened in anticipation at being included in the secret of Joe's newest design.

"I've merely enhanced another element."

"Which is?" Luke asked as Joe paused for a long moment.

"Time," said Joe, and then paused again.

Luke thought about that while the wheels turned. Most people would have immediately asked, "What do you mean?" but Luke thought for himself, and waited to ask the questions that would be most important to help him understand.

"So you use timing to enhance the effect," Luke mused.

"Well, yes, but it's more than that. Music is an awesome accompaniment to a firework display, but if you can get the display to be in time with the music, and have the blasts match the dramatic tempos in the music, you have a more spectacular show. I have merely come up with a way to better control the timing," Joe explained. "I allow the expectation of the audience to help me awe them. I create an expectation, deny it, then give it back again – and they love it."

"So it's like thinking something is over and then being surprised with more," Luke explained.

"Sure," said Joe. "It's like the gum inside a sucker, or jelly in a donut -- something extra that you didn't expect."

"Why hadn't anyone thought of that before?" Luke asked.

"Well they did. I've just come up with a better way to deliver the timing better. That's my secret," said Joe. "It's not just the combination of the same old ingredients. I've added a new ingredient."

"What?" Luke asked eagerly.

They heard a rustling sound behind some crates, and Joe jumped up to investigate, and saw a mouse scurry between two crates.

"Well, I'll tell you one of these days, but it's a huge secret, because it will change the way we manufacture fireworks. It will be worth a lot of money to the person who introduces it – not just prize money, but money on every firework made from here on out," Joe said.

"It's the difference between winning a competition and winning the lottery," he said mimicking Mr. Jacobson's words as he shut the door to the armory behind him, and headed back to the barn.

As they walked across the courtyard, Luke asked, "Hey did you fill out paperwork on the stuff we returned?"

"No. I better go back and do it real quick so I don't forget it tomorrow," Joe replied. "Thanks for reminding me."

As they started back to the abbey, a door opened, and Joe put out his arm to stop Luke. They paused and watched as a dark form emerged from the door that led to the armory. As they shadowy figure approached, Joe stepped forward and said, "Good evening."

The man stopped with a sudden jerk, and then mumbled, "Oh, um – I – uh—didn't know you were there. Shouldn't sneak up on people. Never know when their reflexes will jump into gear."

"Didn't mean to startle you. We were just returning some things that we didn't use tonight," Joe explained, pausing for a response. When there was no response, he asked, "So what brings you to the armory at this late hour?"

"Oh, well, I was just doing a security check. Can't be too careful with explosives. Don't want anything to get away from us, and cause a terrible explosion," he said with a knowing look at Joe.

Joe inhaled sharply, preparing an answer, but Luke broke in, "That's why we're here Mr. Ubsen, we want to make sure our paperwork is complete. Come on, Joe, I want to get back before the dance is over," Luke pulled the reluctant Joe toward the door as Mr. Ubsen went on his way to wherever he was headed so warily in the dark.

"Where did he come from?" Luke asked to change the subject, as he opened the door.

"I wonder," said Joe as he headed behind some crates toward the wall where he'd seen the mouse earlier and examined the floor.

"What're you looking for?" Luke asked.

"Rats," said Joe, glancing around carefully.

"Just don't say that in front of Dori," Luke grinned. "You only have to say the word and she shrieks," he chuckled.

Joe grinned as he straightened up from examining the floor. "Speaking of Dori, we better head back. I promised her a dance."

The two boys made their way downhill to the stable. The sounds of music lit up the night like a blast of lightening brightens a cloudless midnight sky. As they neared the festive crowd, they heard the children squeal with delight as they were included in the dancing.

Logan took his turn with each pretty girl as he made his way around the circle dance. His knees bounced up waist high as his enjoyment of the dance was reflected in each joint and muscle. As he came to one little lady, whose toddler legs were too small to keep up, he swooped her into his arms and twirled her around for her share of fun in the dance. Her eyes glowed with delight as she squealed with glee, before he gently set her on her toes, quickly gave a gentlemanly nod to the little lady, and gaily gave her hand to the next boy in line.

Dori ran to Joe and he cheerfully took his turn as her dance partner, as he led her to the floor for the next dance.

"Mom said I can stay as late as I want. Ben's going to take me home," she said excitedly.

"Well, that might not be such a good idea," Joe said with feigned concern.

"Why not?" Dori asked.

"Well, you know Ben has to get his beauty sleep, and he's sure to go home early," Joe said. "You should have asked me to be your escort," he teased with a grin. "I'll stay as long as the last lantern is lit."

"Well, Mom wanted to leave me with someone sponsible," she said.

"Whoa – oh—oh—are you saying I'm not sponsible?" he mimicked her language lapse.

"Well," she stammered, "There was that one time when I fell asleep in the workshop waiting for you to finish your work, and you went home without me."

"You will never let me forget that will you? Even though I rushed back and got you before you even woke up, and carried you asleep to your bed. You would have never even known about it except for Locomotor-Mouth-Logan," Joe tapped the end of her freckled nose, as she giggled. "Besides I was working on an immensely important project – something that will revolutionize the fireworks industry," he said as he led her off the dance floor as the music ended. "And it's all my idea, that I came up with while you were napping," he said with a grin.

"What is it?" she asked eagerly.

"It's a secret," he said shaking his head and pursing his lips.

"I'm good at keeping secrets," Dori said in a lowered voice.

"Well," said Joe in a hushed voice as he looked around, "It has something to do with salt petre."

"What's that?" asked Dori in a hushed tone with wide eyes.

"It's an explosive used in fireworks," Joe said.

"Is it a secret ingredient?" Dori asked.

"No, but what I do with it is secret," he said with a grin.

"What's that?" Dori asked eagerly.

"I'll tell you later," Joe said. "There might be spies around here," he said looking around furtively.

"Oh, yes," said Dori looking around as Joe crept off on tiptoe with his finger on his lips.

Dori stood for a moment as she contemplated Joe's mystery. She absent-absentmindedly tugged the bow at the end of her pigtail braid. She revived from her daydream as her ribbon dropped to the floor. She bent down to pick it up, and noticed a broken board in the wall. Through the hole was the toe of a worn work boot, with a blackened area the shape of a crescent moon on the toe. She stared at it for a moment, and jumped when the boot shuffled away. Someone had been standing on the other side of the wall, listening to Joe's secret.

"Oh, no. Maybe they heard the secret," whispered Dori. "Maybe it was a spy," she gasped. "I need to find out whose boot that was."

Chapter 5   Brontide Thunder

Suddenly the sound of a loud explosion burst through the air like a cannon blast. The children screamed as they dove for cover from a possible runaway rocket. Even the mothers jumped and spent a moment of brief panic as the realization registered that it was a natural, albeit unexpected phenomenon of a thunderstorm that had created the tremendous noise.

Since the hour was already late, the party was abruptly disbanded as families scurried to safety before the impending downpour. As the instruments were cleaned and hastily put away, Mr. Livingstone hushed the crowd for an announcement.

"Folks, it would be unwise to use the horse-drawn cart with the random lightening strikes, so we are removing the harnesses from the horses and bedding them down for the night in their stalls. Even though the mansion is a quick walk, the lightening strikes are a danger. Fortunately there is a covered walkway leading to the mansion, so if some of you are ready, Logan is prepared to escort you back to your rooms at the mansion. Thank you for a wonderful evening, and we look forward to a great production. Welcome to Rhemawood and the kick-off of this production, and we'll see you tomorrow on the various sets. Good night."

Logan grinned and said, "Follow me," in a voice so lively and cheerful that everyone wanted to go on his adventure. He led them down to the basement of the stable, giving courteous instruction, "Careful of the narrow stairway. Don't bump your ankle on that plow blade. Careful now – go through this doorway." He led them through a stone doorway that looked like part of the foundation of the barn, until he leaned against it, and it swiveled inward revealing a brightly lit passageway.

"Now, please follow me. We'll be at the mansion momentarily," he said, sounding like a tour guide.

The group gave appreciative murmurs of surprise and delight at this new and mysterious close to the evening.

The Livingstone children said their goodbyes to new and old friends in the tunnel under the mansion, and then scurried through the familiar passageway to the cellar of the rookery, racing up the stairs to the kitchen, where they were greeted by mom in her comfy robe, pouring steaming mugs of hot cocoa.

Dori said, "Umm, thanks Mom. I love hot cocoa – Aaagh –," she yelped and jumped as a thunderbolt crashed through the sky outside the kitchen window. Logan laughed at her as she sheepishly and carefully took her mug.

Luke rushed over to the window and opened the curtains hoping for an encore performance.

"Hey, Mom, do you care if we take our mugs upstairs and watch the lightening flashes from there?" Logan asked.

"No. Just bring your mugs down to the kitchen and rinse them out when you're finished," she gently instructed.

"Hey, you guys can come up to the Aerie. The lightening is spectacular from there. You can see it from every direction," Rachael invited.

"Awesome," Logan exclaimed.

Rachael's room was in a tower at the highest point of their home, which was already at the highest point of the mountain. The only way to get to Rachael's room was to go through Dori's room, and pull a handle dangling from the ceiling, which lowered a ladder. Rachael held Dori's mug as she scampered up the ladder. She climbed a few rungs and carefully handed both her mug and Dori's through the hatch door opening, before climbing through herself. The boys balanced their mugs on one hand while climbing the ladder with no hands. Logan wobbled, pretending he was slipping.

"You look like a circus clown, riding a unicycle," Dori giggled.

"Careful guys, hold your mugs; thunder is coming," Rachael

warned as she saw the preceding lightening bolt flash across the sky.

"How do you know?" challenged Dori, then screamed and jumped when the thunder crashed a moment later.

Luke laughed. "Dori, the lightening is a clue to get ready for the thunder. There is always lightening before the thunder. It gives you time to get ready."

"I can tell myself it's coming, and I get ready, but I can't help it. I always jump," Dori said sheepishly.

"Yeah, you get ready all right -- ready to jump in fright," Logan teased as he thundered over her shoulder, laughing as she shrieked.

They all sprawled on the window seats that lined the octagonal tower. Logan, sprawled on his belly with his long legs stretched out, took up one whole side of the tower, as a flash of brilliance lit up the sky, followed quickly by thunder.

"Wow, that one was close," said Luke.

"How can you tell?" Dori asked.

"Well, you count the seconds after a lightening flash until the clap of thunder, and it tells you how far away the strike was," he explained.

"How does it tell you?" asked Dori.

"Well, the lightening bolt is a flash of light, and your eyes can see the light because it travels very fast. The thunder is produced at the same time, but since sound travels slower than light, you hear the thunder later," Luke explained patiently.

"Why does the sound of thunder travel more slowly than light?" asked Logan.

"Well, light is energy and travels in a straight line, whereas sound travels in a wave that goes up and down, taking longer for it to arrive," Luke said, sounding a little bit like a professor.

"Oh," said Dori.

"And what is the difference in the speed?" asked Rachael.

"Well light travels infinitely fast – going around the globe thirty-seven times in five seconds! Sound travels very slowly – only about 768 miles per hour," Luke said.

"Wow. That is slow," Logan said sarcastically. "So that's why you can tell how far away the lightening bolt is, by doing some sort of mathematical calculation based on the speed of sound and the speed of light."

"Precisely," said Luke.

"Yeah, what is the calculation?" asked Logan. "About one mile per second?"

"Actually it is one mile every 4.6 seconds, or about a fifth of a mile per second," Ben said as he poked his head through the floor into the Aerie, so named by Rachael in honor of an eagle's nest high on the utmost crags of a bluff. "Is there room for me?" he asked with a grin.

"Of course," said Rachael, moving some pillows from the seat where they had all been tossed. "Even if we all sprawled out like Logan we could fit two more," Rachael added.

"But what actually turns light into sound?" Logan asked

"Well, the energy of the lightening bolt creates a sudden increase in pressure and temperature, which causes the air to expand rapidly around and within the lightening bolt. The expanding air produces a sonic shock wave," Ben explained.

"Like a sonic boom?" Logan asked.

"Precisely," said Luke.

"What's a sonic boom?" Dori asked.

"It's a series of pressure waves an object creates as it passes through the air, and as the speed of the object increases, the waves are forced together, eventually merging into a single shock wave at the speed of sound, which is mach 1." Luke explained

A low rumble echoed in the tower of the Aerie, and the sound continued to reverberate, at times seeming to fade away, and then increasing its intensity. Rachael looked at Ben in wonder, and Logan, noticing the prolonged thunder asked, "What is that?"

"Listen," said Ben. "Let's see how long it lasts."

The five silently looked at each other as their amazement grew with the length of the rumbling thunder. When it finally subsided, Logan repeated, "What was that?"

"Maybe it was a freight train," said Dori.

"No. It was thunder," said Ben.

"What kind of thunder?" Luke asked.

"It's a special kind of thunder called brontide," Ben explained.

"How far away was that lightening?" Dori asked.

"Well, it would be hard to say," Ben began to explain, "With a regular lightening strike that goes from the sky to the ground, there is a distance, so you can measure the time from lightening flash to thunderclap. With brontide thunder, the electricity of the lightening goes through the air in a horizontal path, and so the bolt of energy isn't just a mile away, it can be traveling several miles across the earth, straight through the air."

"That's why you keep hearing the thunder," Luke said with understanding.

"Why? I don't get it," Logan said in confusion.

"I get it," said Rachael. "If the lightening started here and went several miles east, then we would continue to hear the thunder until the sound waves got too far away."

"Precisely," said Luke.

"I still don't get it," said Dori.

"Here," said Ben. "Let me draw you a picture." He drew a picture of the rookery, and drew a lightening bolt. We see a normal lightening bolt strike the ground one mile away, and 4.6 seconds later we hear the thunder. Another lightening bolt strikes at the same distance horizontally and travels through the air for fifty miles. We begin to hear the thunder 4.6 seconds after the strike, and we continue hearing sound waves, and until it gets about 12-15 miles away."

"Plus 4.6 seconds," said Luke.

"Right," said Ben, as he handed the picture to Dori.

"So what causes lightening to strike in a way that causes brontide thunder?" Rachael asked.

"Well, I guess just the way the energy travels through space," said Ben.

"Why do they call it Brontide?" asked Luke.

"Well, bronto means thunder, like Brontosaurus means 'thunder lizard'," Logan said, "And I bet it has something to do with Brontes."

"What is that?" asked Dori.

"He was one of the sons of Uranus and Gaia, in Greek mythology," explained Logan, a great admirer of literature.

"Yeah. They were one-eyed giants," said Rachael.

"Cyclops," said Logan. He covered one eye, and crossed the other toward his nose as he lumbered like an ogre toward Dori.

"Oooh," squealed Dori.

"They kind of had a dysfunctional family, like most of the Greek mythical heroes, didn't they?" Rachael asked Logan.

"Yeah. There were three brothers, Arges, Steropes and Brontes. Their father was jealous of them, and afraid they might dethrone him, so he locked them up in the underworld, until Zeus, the ruler of the sky, freed them. They made thunderbolts for Zeus at their forge. Arges added brightness, Brontes added thunder, and Steropes added lightening. In fact, they created three instruments of mythological power: Zeus' thunderbolts, Poseidon's trident, and Hades' helmet of darkness."

They talked Greek mythology for a while, until they began to get sleepy. Luke offered to take the mugs to the kitchen, and the others climbed down and went to bed, calling a goodnight to Rachael. She let down her bed by pulling a rope attached to pulleys that slowly lowered her bed from the ceiling, revealing a skylight where she could continue to watch the natural fireworks display that continued for her enjoyment in the sky after she climbed under the covers. She listened in comfort to the echoing thunder surrounding her comfy little nest.

Chapter 6   Beware!

Midnight darkness clothed the mountain in mystique. The black sky was an omen foretelling a mystery. Thunder roared its anger as the lightening flashes revealed a momentary clue before plunging the mountain into the darkness of deception.

The Livingstone children slept safe in the security of the rookery, while the storm raged all around, but the thunder proclaimed a warning, hinting at a mystery that the lightening was unable to reveal. Luke bolted upright in bed as he heard a voice so deep that its bass tones echoed in his chest, "Beware!"

As Luke's eyes adjusted to the darkness, the echoes of ominous warning reverberated in the silent room. He looked around for the voice that had awakened him. It wasn't Dad's voice or his brothers', or even a human voice, and yet it wasn't a remnant of a dream. He looked over at Joe, sleeping peacefully in his bed. Fully awake, he wandered across the hallway into the room Ben and Logan shared.

Logan was sprawled on the top berth of the three-tiered bunk, legs askew, and one arm hanging over the bunk. Ben was tucked neatly in his bunk, like a tidy naval officer. Luke observed all was well as a lightening bolt lit up the room. He mentally counted the seconds until a thundering sound rattled the walls, "Caution," it seemed to shout in the same voice that had awakened him earlier.

Luke rubbed his eyes, shook his head, and wandered back to his bed. The thunderstorm was trying to warn him of what? As he drifted off to sleep, one low rumble shouted, "Warning!" from a distance as the storm left the mountainside.

The next thing Luke heard was Ben's voice, "Hey, want to go with me to find Joe? He's not in the house, and so he's probably at the abbey already. I told him I'd help him this morning, but I hope you can help me find the right tunnel."

Luke leaped out of bed onto one foot, while the other was slipping on a shoe. "Sure," he said with excitement. Luke always loved a great adventure, and he didn't want to miss a minute.

Ben laughed, "Get dressed first. I'll meet you in the kitchen."

Two minutes later Luke and Ben were in the tunnel under the rookery racing up the stairs to the abbey. From this tunnel you could get to several places on the mountaintop, and the Livingstone children frequently came to the abbey through the tunnel. The abbey contained several old brick buildings surrounding a cobblestone courtyard.

They headed for the building where they'd taken the leftover fireworks last night. When they opened the door, they saw a light on, but no one in sight.

Ben began to straighten up the desk, which had managed to get cluttered again, and Luke examined some of the crates of rockets and ingredients for making fireworks. He intently studied a label, and asked Ben, "Hey, what's the chemical notation for potassium nitrate?"

"KNO_3," a voice replied over his shoulder. Luke flinched slightly, turned his head, and said, "Hey, where'd you come from?"

"Oh, just exploring," Joe said vaguely.

Luke looked around suspiciously, letting his eyes rest on the floor behind Joe, where he'd examined it the night before. "Find any rats?" he asked.

"Yeah, a big fat one with a long tail," he said distractedly. "Come on. Let's get to work," he said abruptly changing the subject.

"Why didn't you wake me?" Ben asked.

"I knew you'd get here right on time," Joe said vaguely. "We have a lot to do before everyone else gets ready. The special effects for this production are awesome, and I need you to help me pull it all together."

Ben and Luke busily followed Joe's advice as he barked orders like a drill sergeant. As the sun began to rise in the east, Joe's cell phone rang, and he teased as he answered the call, "Did you decide to sleep in, Dad?"

Dad chuckled a wide-awake, "No. I've had breakfast, and put together some production notes, and was just going to wake you when I found all the bunks deserted except for one."

"Yeah. The guys are here with me, and you're on speaker phone."

"You want me to wake Logan up?" Dad asked.

"Nah. Let him sleep in, and he can meet up with us later and bring the girls," Joe said.

"Okay," said Dad. "Joe, I need to go over some production notes with you for today. I'm meeting with the crew at the conference room at the mansion for breakfast at 7:00. Just meet us there."

"Okay," said Joe. "See you there. Gotta go!" He said as he shut the phone and said to his brothers, "Come on guys – if I'm going to make it to the production meeting, we better get a move on."

"If?" Ben asked.

"I've got to get one last item that isn't at the armory. It'll make a spectacular effect today," Joe said with excitement.

"Come on." He led the way to the abbey library, and wove his way through several rows of bookshelves until he came to a secluded corner.

Luke ran his hands over a row of books and said, "Wow – look at these old books on Chinese fireworks. No wonder you like this section, Joe."

"You would really like the big volume with purple binding and gold letters," Joe said.

"This one?" Luke asked as he slid it from the row of rich, colorful volumes. The book was stuck and as Luke tugged the spine of the book, the bookshelf suddenly swung toward them, revealing a tunnel behind it.

"Oh, cool," said Luke. "A new tunnel."

"Is this the tunnel you used to explore when you were at Rhemawood before?" Ben asked.

"The very one. Follow me," Joe said with excitement. The tunnel walls soon became the rough rocky walls of a cave as they descended into the cool depths of the earth.

"Did you explore very far?" Luke asked.

"Yeah. I made a map of several tunnels," Joe said, "But I didn't go nearly as far as I would have liked, only because I knew Mom wouldn't like me going too far."

"Yeah, but she would be okay with you going into a hidden tunnel, descending into a cave, and exploring it to make a map?" asked Luke.

"Well, it is sort of like geography – anyway I just never got around to asking her," Joe said sheepishly.

"What are we looking for anyway?" Ben asked.

"Guano," said Joe.

"What do you want bat manure for?" asked Luke.

"It's an ingredient in the explosion I'm planning for today. It will make the flame more spectacular," Joe explained.

"How so?" asked Luke.

"Well, you remember the flame test we talked about yesterday?"

"Yeah. That is so cool," Luke said.

"Yeah, it is, but I need potassium nitrate to produce the color flame that I want today," Joe explained.

"And what is that color?" Luke asked.

"A cool lilac color. Potassium nitrate produces a unique lilac, and I want that for today's special effect."

"But Mr. Ubsen said we don't have any potassium nitrate," Luke said.

"Well, then we have to get it from another source," said Joe. "It pays to know your chemistry, and what natural ingredients contain which elements. It just so happens that potassium nitrate can be found occurring naturally."

"Bat guano," Luke said with a nod.

"Precisely," Joe said mimicking Luke's professor voice.

"Cool. So where is the bat colony?" asked Luke.

"I don't know," Joe said.

"Well, look at your map," said Ben.

"I don't have my map. It's hidden with my other secret stash. I just remember seeing a few bats when I was here before, and where there are bats, there is guano," he said confidently.

Ben looked nervously at his watch. "We don't really have time to just wander around looking for a bat colony. The production meeting starts in twenty minutes."

"Quit worrying. We'll make it," Joe said confidently.

"Well, it took us four minutes to get here, and accounting for time to get back, that leaves us twelve minutes more to find the bat guano and race to the production meeting," Ben calculated.

"Look! There's a bat on the ceiling," Joe said triumphantly. "We're getting close. I know it. You know I'm always right," he said.

"Yeah, but I know you're also always late," Ben retorted.

"Tell you what – you go to the production meeting and get there early, like you always do, and Luke and I will get the guano, and show up right in the nick of time," Joe said.

"All right," Ben said unconvinced, but already heading back to the library.

After another ten minutes, Luke recommended heading to the production meeting. "We're already gonna be a few minutes late," he cautioned Joe.

"Oh, come on, Luke. Where's your sense of adventure? This

ingredient will make the difference between a so-so explosion and a spectacular special effect," he cajoled.

"Yeah, but you know Dad values promptness more than spectacular," said Luke.

"No way. He'll be so impressed he'll give me a promotion," Joe boasted. "Come on. Just a little further." The tunnel was widening into a large cavern, and Joe whispered, "See? Pay dirt."

Luke shook his head. How did Joe always know? Sure enough, piles of bat guano lined the cavern, and after scooping a bucketful, Joe and Ben hurried back to the library.

They raced through the tunnel, and up the steps that began at the mansion furnace room, and Luke led Joe down the hallway to a large conference room where about forty people were seated at tables, the remnants of pastries on their plates while they sipped the last cool dregs of coffee. Luke recognized Mr. Ubsen, who raised his eyebrows in reproof at their late arrival.

As they sat down, their father, who stood at the front of the room, with the eager and respectful attention of the crew, made a closing statement. "So, keep in mind the safety instructions, refer to the schedule if you have any questions, and let's make this a productive day." There was a scurrying as the room emptied quickly, while the team scattered to their jobs.

As Ben gathered his notes, Joe walked over and said, "Where do we head first, Ben?" Dad looked up from a conversation he was having with one of the crew supervisors, and said, "Joe, I'm sorry you missed the meeting, but it might be best if Mr. Ubsen headed the effects today. He knows what we need already, and timing is essential."

"Aw, Dad. Come on. I'm ready. I can handle it. You know I'm the best one for this job. No one can do it better. . ."

"Son, I'm not questioning your talent, but there are a lot of details you missed," Dad continued.

"I've got a new formula I'm going to put together for today that will make a more colorful explosion," Joe told Dad excitedly.

"That sounds great, Joe, but it's more important to get this first effect completed on schedule. You can take some time later to specialize the effect, but I want this first one to go smoothly," Dad explained.

Luke noticed Mr. Ubsen standing smugly at the coffee pot, slowly getting a refill while he listened for other juicy morsels of a conversation that he wasn't invited to.

"Ben can fill me in. Can't you ole buddy?" Joe said as he put his arm around Ben's shoulder. "Come on, Dad," Joe wheedled.

Dad hesitated and said, "Okay, get the production notes from Ben. But Joe," Dad paused to make sure he had Joe's full attention, "You need to make sure everything goes well today. The safety of the cast and crew depend on it, and I need to know

I can count on you to be part of the team."

"No worries," Joe said, laughing as he turned away. "Where to first, Benny Boy?" Joe asked pleased with his success.

Luke noticed Dad watching Joe, with pursed lips, and wrinkled brow, as when he was concerned, but then he was quickly distracted by another question from a crewmember, and Luke almost bumped into Mr. Ubsen, who was also watching Joe with squinty eyes. "What was he up to?" Luke wondered.

Chapter 7 Orpheus' Muse

Rachael finished up the breakfast dishes just as Logan wandered into the kitchen, "Hey, where is everybody?" he demanded sleepily.

"Everybody has eaten breakfast and started their day except for you, Sleepyhead," Rachael said, cocking one eye at Logan's wild hair.

"Why didn't anybody wake me up?" he howled.

"Mom said that everyone could sleep in today if they wanted since we were up so late last night," Rachael explained as she dried the last dish.

"Well, how come no one else is in bed?" Logan demanded.

"I guess they had important things to do," Rachael said with a superior air.

"Without me?" he demanded indignantly.

"Well, I happen to know where they might be. Do you want to help me find them? It could be an adventure," she said with a tempting grin.

"Sure," said Logan, grabbing an apple and a bagel.

"Wait for me," yelled Dori racing down the kitchen stairs from the attic where she had been playing.

"Follow me," said Rachael, grabbing a backpack next to the kitchen door.

"Where are we going?" asked Logan.

"You'll see," she said with a grin. She headed across the yard and stopped at the boulder where they had emerged from the tunnel with Joe the day before.

"Well?" said Logan as he waited for her lead. "What are you waiting for?"

"I'm not sure how to open the door," Rachael said sheepishly. "We'll have to figure that out."

"Where's Luke when you need him?" muttered Logan.

"Open Sesame!" Dori shouted.

Rachael laughed, "There has to be a mechanism to open the door – a lever or switch or something." She looked all around the boulder and Logan clambered on top of it to search.

"Maybe it is a pressure sensitive switch, and when you press it, the rock swings open," he said.

"Walk around and see if you trigger something," she called to Logan. He started to walk gingerly at first, searching for a knob or button, but since it was a large boulder, he decided to cover more ground by hopping around with his high jerky knee steps that passed for dancing. Dori giggled.

"All right. Obviously there's no switch on the boulder. Maybe it's a motion sensor. Come down here and dance around," Rachael grinned. Logan leaped to the ground, grabbed Dori's hands and swung her around the perimeter of the boulder as he said with a country twang, "Grab yer pardner and do-so-do." Dori squealed with laughter.

"Don't think that's working either," said Rachael, "Although it's highly amusing to watch."

Logan dropped Dori's hands, and she flopped to the ground, dizzied by the dance.

"Ow!" she yelped, and looked down. "Hey – I think I found something." Hidden by the thick green grass and ivy that surrounded the base of the boulder was a small metal foot pedal. Dori was too small to push it down, but Logan stepped on it, and they heard a click and the boulder swung out, revealing the passageway.

"Come on," he shouted as he ran into the tunnel. As he came to a Y in the tunnel, he abruptly stopped, and Dori barreled into him. "Where are we going anyway?" he asked.

"Well, it is important to know where you're going when you're the leader," Rachael said sarcastically.

"Oh – sorry," Logan said sheepishly, bowing slightly with his arm outstretched to offer her the lead.

Rachael chuckled, "To tell you the truth, I'm not sure where I'm going either." Logan's jaw dropped in pretended shock. "But, I know this tunnel leads to the caverns, and I suspect that we can get to the Orpheum from the cave passageways."

"Is that where everyone is?" Logan asked.

"I think that's where the action is," Rachael replied.

"Well, let's go then," said Logan, retaking the lead now that he had some direction. They retraced the path they had taken with Joe, and came out on the mountaintop where they had hidden from Luke the day before.

"Race you to the Orpheum," Logan called, loping with a sideways step down the steep hillside to keep his balance.

"Careful, Dori," Rachael called as Dori followed Logan cautiously.

As they rounded the hill, they saw the large sign in intricate scrollwork that said, "Orpheum."

"What's Orpheum?" Dori asked.

"It's a large theater, taken from the name Orpheus, a mythological character who supposedly created music. The large Greek Amphitheaters were named after Orpheus." As Logan explained this literature trivia fact, they wandered into the mouth of the cave. "Hey, where is everybody?" Logan demanded. "Hello! Hello!" he shouted, and his voice echoed off the walls of the huge cavern.

The risers, chairs, and music stands were arranged like silent soldiers in the orchestra pit, but the musicians had abandoned their post.

"Where now?" Logan demanded.

"Why don't we explore the cave?" Dori asked.

"Dad said we could as long as we follow the caving protocol," Logan added.

"And I've got the supplies already," Rachael concluded, patting her backpack.

"Yes!" Logan shouted as he shoved his hand into the backpack and grabbed the radio. He pushed the button, and said, "Logan Livingstone to home base. Do you copy?" There was a brief pause as they waited.

"Copy. What is your location?" replied a professional voice.

"Hey, Mom. How are you this morning?" Logan grinned, lapsing from his normal radio voice.

"Fine, Son." Mom laughed, then continued. "Repeat. What is your location?"

"Oh – sorry—Rachael, Dori and I are at the Orpheum." He grabbed the GPS unit from the backpack. "Our precise coordinates are – "

"Never mind," said Rachael. "She knows where this is."

"Oh – right," Logan replied.

Rachael held out her hand for the radio. "Hey Mom, we'd like to explore the caverns. We're going to enter at the opening in the hillside above the Orpheum, Joe knows where it is, and we'd like to see where it goes in the cave. Is that okay?"

"Sure. Just –" (and here Logan mouthed the words with her to Dori with a grin) – "follow the safety protocol."

"We will," said Rachael. "We'll check in and give you our coordinates from time to time."

"Do you have an extra flashlight?" Mom asked.

"Two extra!" said Rachael.

"Have fun!" Mom said.

Logan reached over and pressed the button. "Roger. Over and out," he grinned as mom replied, "Over and out!"

They climbed the steep hill and switched on their flashlights as they went behind the boulder and down the stone steps into the earth. The cave meandered through a rock-lined corridor. Cold cave water occasionally plunked on their heads, and onto the damp floor. They grew silent as they flashed their lights around the cave.

"Look – there's a bat," Logan whispered as he flashed his light toward the cave ceiling. Dori shivered slightly.

"I hope we don't run into Orpheus," Dori replied in a whisper.

Logan laughed, "Well, if you ever wanted to meet Orpheus, this would be the place. Have I ever told you the whole story, Dori?"

"No," she answered.

"Maybe this isn't the best time or place," Rachael cautioned.

"No, I want to hear it," Dori pleaded, taking a seat on a stone ledge.

Logan took the flashlight, and pointed it upward under his chin. It made him look like a disembodied ghoul as the shadows moved eerily across his face, while he began his tale in an ominous voice. "Well, Orpheus was the son of Calliope, a muse."

"What's a muse?" asked Dori.

Logan struck a pose, like one of Shakespeare's players of the stage, and quoted, "Well, Hesiod, the Greek poet said, The Muses "are all of one mind, their hearts are set upon song and their spirit is free from care. He is happy whom the Muses love. For though a man has sorrow and grief in his soul, yet when the servant of the Muses sings, at once he forgets his dark thoughts and remembers not his troubles. Such is the holy gift of the Muses to men," Logan quoted in a wonderful and theatrical voice.

He continued, "Orpheus played beautiful music on his harp. It was so beautiful that it could tame wild beasts and make grass grow, and flowers bloom. He fell in love with a nymph named Euridice, but on their wedding day, she was bitten by a poisonous snake and died."

"How sad," Dori said.

"Orpheus' grief was so intense that he traveled the

underworld to find her, and his music charmed even the three-headed beast of Hades. The mythical rulers of the underworld allowed Euridice to follow him back to life, but he had to agree to not look at her until they were safely back in the sunlight."

"What happened?" Dori asked breathlessly.

"Oh, they lived happily ever after," Rachael said.

"Huh uh," said Logan, perturbed. "It is a tragic Greek myth, full of intrigue and suspense."

"Well, maybe Dori would like to hear about the tragic intrigue and suspense later – in the sunlight," Rachael strongly hinted.

"No, really – I'd like to hear it," said Dori.

"All right," Rachael sighed, slipping down beside Dori on the narrow ledge, with a boulder for a backrest.

"Well," continued Logan with a voice fraught with suspense, "Orpheus was traveling through the tunnels of the underworld, a tunnel just like this one, strumming his harp. He hoped Euridice was following him, but he couldn't turn and look because of the deal he had made with Hades. He thought he heard footsteps, but was it Euridice, or a demon sent by Hades to destroy him?"

Here Logan paused for dramatic effect.

Suddenly Dori gasped with an intake of breath, "Do you hear that?" she whispered.

"What?" Rachael asked.

"I hear harp music. Do you?" Dori asked.

Logan laughed, pleased at the success of his story, until he saw the look on Rachael's face. "What?" he demanded.

"Shhh. Listen," she commanded.

The sounds of plucking strings and a melodious song of a harp echoed through the cavern. "It's probably the orchestra tuning up, and their song is flowing through the cave like yesterday," Logan explained.

Dori stood up on the ledge, turned around, and peeked over the boulder that had been the backrest behind her. Above the boulder was an opening, and it overlooked a large cavern below. It was as though they were in a balcony of a theater, looking down on the main auditorium. The harp music was coming from that cavern, which was lit by many lights.

Rachael gasped as a man dressed in a Greek toga, carrying and strumming an old fashion lyre appeared. He wore sandals on his feet, and his golden curls were entwined with laurel and flowers. He played a haunting melody and as he moved through the cavern below, a shadow appeared behind him. He paused, as though wanting to look behind, but willed himself to continue walking. He made his way slowly across the cavern, followed by the echo of soft footfalls, but the kids could see nothing but an occasional shadow, like a flowing, fluttering gown.

As the young musician left the cavern, and the trailing echo of footsteps faded, suddenly a large three-headed beast burst from the shadows and gave a ferocious and menacing growl from one head, while another sniffed the air, and the third found the scent on the ground and the beast furtively followed the handsome harp player and his invisible partner. Rachael put her hand over Dori's mouth to stifle the scream and rushed her back down the tunnel. Logan was heading the opposite way to find the beast, but Rachael grabbed his arm and dragged him along, too.

As they returned hastily to the sunlight, Logan sputtered, "What's the big idea? That might have been my only chance to discover the three-headed beast of Hades and Greek mythology."

"Maybe tomorrow, Homer," said Rachael as she turned to check on Dori.

Chapter 8 Brontes' Forge

"Okay, Ben, I need ten grams of sodium nitrate, and fill this with bat guano," Joe said as he intently measured ingredients into a paper shell.

Ben hurriedly filled the container, handed it to Joe, and said carefully, "Joe, Dad said not to waste time enhancing the special effect. We really need to be on-site making final preparations. We have to be set up by 10:00, and we still have to complete a safety inspection," Ben said with concern.

"Stop worrying, Ben. Don't I always pull through?" Joe said confidently.

Luke looked at Ben's face, as he checked his watch, and realized Ben was not convinced this time.

Joe threaded the fuse into the casing, capped it off with some clay, and said triumphantly, "See? All done. Let's go, slow pokes," he said to Ben and Luke as he took the lead.

"Aren't you going to test it first?" Ben asked.

"Nah," Joe replied. "I know what I'm doing," he said confidently.

Luke noticed that Ben's already worried face looked even more concerned, but he had complete confidence in Joe, and was excited to be part of the special effects crew today. They made their way to the set.

As they rounded a corner, they almost bumped into Mr. Ubsen, who said, "Where ya been? We're almost ready for you."

✗

What kind of beast was that?" Dori asked breathlessly.

"It was the three-headed beast of Hades," said Logan excitedly.

"Yeah, but what's it doing in our caverns?" asked Rachael.

"I don't know, but I'd sure like to find out," Logan said heading back into the cave entrance.

"Do you think it's safe?" Rachael asked.

"Let's just go take a quick look," Logan said.

"Maybe we should check in with Mom first," Rachael cautioned.

"Are you kidding? She'll say no, and then we won't have any fun," said Logan.

"Well, then maybe we shouldn't be doing it," Rachael lectured.

Logan rolled his eyes as he got out the radio and called, "Logan to base. Come in base."

"Roger. Base," a voice replied.

"Hey, Mom, we'd like to go back in the same tunnel to explore a little further." He paused and looked at Rachael, who nodded her head for him to continue. "We thought we saw Orpheus and Euridice, and the three-headed beast from Hades, and we just want to give it a closer look," he shrugged his shoulders at Rachael while he paused and waited for Mom to negate their fun.

"Roger that," said Mom. "If you see them, tell them we're having sandwiches and salad for lunch today in the Orpheum."

Logan raised his eyes in wonder and said, "Uh – sure," then he quickly said, "Over and out," and took his finger off the button. "You heard her. Come on," he said as he headed to the tunnel.

"Evidently it wasn't a good connection," Rachael explained, following hesitantly as Dori grabbed her hand.

They quietly made their way back to the balcony and looked over the boulder to the open cavern below. The cavern was dark and silent, "Well, they might be long gone, but let's see if we can find our way down and take a look around," said Logan.

"Are you sure it's safe?" Dori asked.

"Sure," said Logan. "If the beast comes back, I'll throw it my peanut butter sandwich," he grinned.

"You better break it into three pieces," Dori cautioned.

"Yeah, and throw the pieces in different directions, while we run the other way," Rachael said as Dori giggled at the thought of the three-headed beast fighting with itself over which direction to go for the peanut butter sandwich pieces.

"Come on. This way," Logan whispered, following the tunnel trail as it went down.

They climbed between boulders and down natural stone steps, and came to the bottom of the large cavern.

"Shhh—do you hear that?" Rachael asked.

Clanking noises echoed from way down one tunnel.

"What is it?" Dori asked.

"It sounds like a hammer," Rachael said.

"Maybe it is a miner with his pick, searching for gold," Dori suggested.

"Let's go see," said Logan, and Rachael reluctantly followed with Dori gripping her hand.

As they got closer, the blows became louder. "Sounds like metal on metal," Logan said. "Almost like an anvil," he mused. As they turned a corner Logan put his hand out to stop the girls, and pulled them back against the cave wall, but not before they saw a huge barrel-chested man with a patch over one eye. Clothed in a leather apron, he stood at a forge which glowed red hot, and even more so as he stepped on a peddle and blew air from the bellows into the flame, making the fire brilliantly red.

With a massive set of tongs, he pulled a glowing iron stake from the coals, set it on his anvil and struck it with his huge hammer. Sparks flew as the metal took shape under the fierce blows of the sledge.

The children stood watching silently as he took another piece of metal and under extreme heat, welded it to the first one, bending and striking to make it take shape. The tool now had two prongs and he took one more piece of metal to attach to the end, fashioning a three-pronged tool, like a pitchfork.

Logan pulled Dori and Rachael back into the tunnel, and when they were far enough back he said, "I think it's Brontes," he said excitedly.

"You mean the ruler of thunder?" Dori yelped.

"No. Zeus is the mythical ruler of thunder. Brontes created thunderbolts for Zeus. He also fashioned the trident for Poseidon. I think that's what he's making now," Logan said excitedly.

"I think you're right," said Rachael. "Do you think he's safe to watch?" she asked.

"I don't think he can see us from this angle with that patch over his eye," said Logan. "Let's watch him some more." As they maneuvered back into place a thunderous sound exploded from the underworld, and reverberated through the tunnels.

"Brontes," a voice that sounded like many waters echoed from the cavern tunnel. It was gushing, flowing, and rapidly racing, rushing toward a waterfall cascading into a deep pool where the flow was encompassed in the depths of old.

Brontes responded with a one-syllable grunt that was enforced by the hammer striking the anvil.

"Brontes," the voice repeated, and now as thunder always accompanies lightening, the source of the voice appeared in a flash of brilliance. He was a large being with long cascading locks of hair whitened by age and wisdom, merging with the white beard to form a cloak of white feathery fur around his shoulders. A garment of shimmering blues flowed to the floor. It was impossible to tell where the beard became fabric.

As a launderer knows, you can whiten white by adding blue dye to the rinse water. As the sky can attest, white can become blue without a dividing line of distinction. Can you tell where the clouds end and sky begins on a certain day when the sky is cloud blue – or the clouds are sky white? So was this garment, which was white at the top and as blue as the depths of the ocean at the bottom, as waves of fabric rolled in seamless flow while this great figure sailed into view.

"Brontes – my trident – is it complete?"

Again the strike of the hammer answered.

"You must add the power of thunder to my trident just as you did for the thunderbolts of Zeus."

A flash of light appeared and instantly a clap of thunder, and from the smoke a voice pierced the darkness of a cavern tunnel.

As the voice echoed and pulsated with power, so did the image as it began to appear slowly as a pulsating energy of darkness took shape in the shadows.

"Beware of the power of the thunder," the voice boomed out of the energy of a storm. As the voice continued to speak, the outline of a form appeared much like a thundercloud appears in the night sky, a voluminous mass of black and gray illuminated from behind by invisible starlight.

"The power of thunder is its pride, but the real strength resides in the lightening," the first voice replied.

"Thunder is only a dark and invisible reflection of the energy of light. Thunder is what remains after the power of the light is gone – an impotent testimony of the truth cloaked in a deceitful shout of defiance. Its only real power is in inciting fear."

"And yet even though invisible, fear is powerful. So the power of thunder is in the fear it inspires. Fear begets fear, and multiplies as it feeds on itself," the second form expanded into an immense cloud of doom and darkness as it spoke.

"Zeus, my friend," the voice of waters splashed merrily in the darkened cavern.

"Yes, my old friend and brother, Poseidon, our power lies in our ability to frighten and intimidate our subjects – to keep them in the dark, away from the one question that might allow them to free themselves from the power of our thunder."

"How powerful is thunder without lightening?" asked

Poseidon.

"And where does the dark go when the light appears?" Zeus queried.

"How true. The power is in the light, not in the thundering darkness," Poseidon answered. "And yet, witness the power of my thunder bolt." He raised his thunderbolt, clenched in his hand, and a lightening bolt shot forth into the forge of Brontes. There was a flash of light, and an explosion. Sparks flew everywhere. Rachael pulled Dori down, and covered her with her body. Logan leaned over to shield the girls, but couldn't take his eyes off the action.

He saw a red coal land on Brontes' hand, and watched him grimace in pain, trying not to show his anguish. As the sparks stopped flying, a loud voice shouted, "Cut. First aid to Brontes."

Immediately lights came on, the camera crew pulled back, and the cavern was illuminated, revealing a world that had been hidden in shadows. The crew scurried to their assigned roles in a flurry of activity, and a first aid kit was dispatched and ointment applied to Brontes.

"Check the shot to make sure you don't have the kids in the frame," Dad said to the cameraman, nodding to Logan, Dori and Rachael. "Let's all break for lunch at the Orpheum, and meet back here at 1:00," he called. He took a quick look at Brontes' burn, and then headed to Joe with a serious look on his face.

He pulled Joe aside, but Rachael could hear what he said,

even though she wished she hadn't. "Joe, I don't know what went wrong with that special effect, but it should have been a simple flash of light, not enough to throw coals and burn one of my actors. We got lucky this time, but I want you to take a few days to get your head on straight. Do your own thing and take a break for a day or two. You're not invested in this production like I need, and after you've had a few days to settle in, then maybe we'll see if you can be a productive member of this team," he said sternly.

"But, Dad—" Joe started to say, but when he saw the look on Dad's face, he fell silent.

Dad said, "I need to go. We can talk more at home." He headed back to give instructions to the rest of the crew.

Joe looked with disbelief after his father, and then grabbed a flashlight from his pocket, turned on his heel, and strode down the tunnel. Logan called after him, "Hey, Joe, wait for me," but Joe didn't look back. Logan started to follow him, but decided to stay in the caverns. As he turned to go back to Rachael and Dori, he almost bumped into the shadowy figure of Mr. Ubsen, and noticed an odd look of triumph on his face at the failure of Joe's special effect. Ben and Luke stood awkwardly silent, but did not follow Joe.

Chapter 9   It Ain't Braggin' if You Done It!

Joe sat in his lab surrounded by scales and beakers and Bunsen burners. This was a world that was predictable; a set of known components always produced an expected outcome. Luke found Joe perched on a lab stool, hunched over his workbench, with his safety goggles in place.

He walked quietly into the room, and took a seat on a lab stool, and waited for Joe to notice him. He had learned long ago that to be a welcome companion to Joe, he must be willing to quietly observe. When Joe was contemplating a new design, or completing a mathematical conversion for a chemical formula, or observing a chemical reaction while writing notes, silence was essential and distraction could be disastrous.

So Luke ate his sandwich, set Joe's lunch on the counter and quietly observed his older brother, and in his silence was affirming his fidelity. Luke didn't know anyone who was as accomplished as Joe. All of his siblings were smart, but Joe knew how to take all that head knowledge and turn it into something you could see and touch. Anyone could memorize the periodic table, but Joe actually understood the elements, and how they fit together like invisible puzzle pieces to create something new and tangible.

Finally Joe looked up and said, "Wouldn't you rather be where the action is?"

"I've always discovered that wherever you are is where the action is," Luke said sincerely. "I brought your lunch," he said nodding to the package on the lab counter.

"Thanks. It's pretty quiet here today – no explosions or anything like in the caverns," Joe said.

"If it's good enough for you, it's good enough for me," Luke said loyally.

"That's the point – it's not good enough. That's why I'm here and Dad is using Mr. Ubsen."

"He's not anywhere near as good as you, Joe," Luke protested loyally. "He doesn't even know how to pronounce pyrotechnics."

Joe looked evenly at Luke. "Dad knows best, and if he says Mr. Ubsen is best, then there is a reason. I just need to discover what the reason is."

Luke looked down in silence, knowing Joe was right.

"I've been sitting here trying to create a mathematical equation to discover what Mr. Ubsen has that I don't, and I can't get it to work out. Even using 'n' as an unknown number, I can't see that he can offer anything to the production that I can't."

"When I can't solve an algebraic equation, it's usually because I've omitted a negative integer," Luke joked.

Joe looked thoughtful. "You're right. It might not be that Mr. Ubsen has anything extra – maybe he is just missing something I have that is negative to my side of the equation," Joe surmised. "Wonder what that could be? Talent, skill, inventiveness," Joe continued his list sarcastically, but with an element of truth, as they both knew.

"Pride," Luke said drolly, rolling his eyes.

The truth of Luke's words came to them both like a flash of lightening, striking the truth, and exposing it in brilliance.

"Confidence is a good thing," Joe protested, then added quietly, "But arrogance is not a virtue, I suppose."

"Why not?" Luke asked. "If it's true that you are better with pyrotechnics, why shouldn't everyone know it. As Dizzy Dean said, "It ain't braggin if you can do it.""

Joe replied thoughtfully, "Well, perhaps truth and pride are like oil and water and they don't mix well."

"So, just because you're the best doesn't mean you should take pride in it," Luke explained.

"Let another praise you and not thine own lips," Joe quoted an old proverb. "I suppose like everything, there is a balance, and I have to discover where confidence ends and arrogance begins," Joe contemplated.

"Can I help?" Luke asked.

"I think I'm going to have to figure this one out on my own – but I'll sure let you know if I need you," Joe said. "Thanks for lunch, Luke," he said with a grateful nod. "I've got a lot of thinking to do. Why don't you head to the set?"

Luke nodded and gave Joe a brotherly pat on his shoulder as he left.

Luke was distracted as he walked across the courtyard of the abbey. He decided to slip into the library before heading back to the movie set. Books were always comforting friends to Luke, and this library was filled from floor to ceiling with shelves heavy with books. If you stood in the center of the room you could look up through five levels of the library. This building was one of the tallest structures of the abbey, built on a corner of the enclosed compound. From the outside it looked like a lookout tower for the small village, which also included a stone chapel, classrooms and dormitories, all connected with covered walkways with a central courtyard. From outside the walls, the abbey looked like a huge brick and stone structure with a tower at one corner – the library.

Luke stood at the center of the library tower, and looked up at each level. The center got narrower until the top was just a four-sided balcony surrounded by windows that allowed the sunlight to filter in rays of dust laden pathways to the ancient books below.

Luke climbed the staircase to the top level of the library, a cupola that rose from the top of the tower like a sentry. This level contained no books, but consisted of a seat ledge bordering each side of windows on the outer edge, and a balcony around the inner edge. From here, you could look all the way down to the floor of the library. Luke wandered around the perimeter of the balcony, looking out the windows. From the windows, the view of Rhemawood was awesome.

On one side he could see the mansion. As he walked to the other side he could look to the rookery and see Miss Sophia's tower peeking over the other side of the mountaintop. As he continued to the other side he could look out over the woods of the mountainside, and the roofs of the abbey buildings. Coming to the final side he could look down into the courtyard of the abbey. He looked to the pathways and miniature shrubbery below. He saw Mr. Ubsen come out of the armory door and walk furtively across the courtyard, toward Joe's workshop. Then Joe and Mr. Ubsen walked together back to the armory.

After a minute they came back out of the armory and Joe went back to his workshop as Mr. Ubsen began to walk through the courtyard. He glanced back toward Joe's workshop and then furtively retraced his steps to the armory. Luke waited for him to come out again, and when he didn't reappear he descended the stairs and wandered back to Joe's workshop.

"Hey, Joe, I'm heading back to the cavern – change your mind and want to come?"

"No, thanks," Joe replied.

"Hey – what did Mr. Ubsen want?"

"Oh, Dad sent him to get the Flying Flambé'. Guess he wants to use it as part of an effect today," Joe said dejectedly.

"Isn't that your special entry for the national festival?" Luke asked.

"Yep."

"Why would Dad want to use that?" Luke asked.

"I don't know. Guess he has his reasons." Joe said somberly.

"Yeah, but he would want you to handle the effects," Luke said.

"Dad knows what he's doing," Joe said resignedly.

"Yeah, but does Mr. Ubsen?" Luke muttered to himself. To Joe he said, "Aren't you even curious to see how it works out?"

"I'd really rather not be there if I'm not helping," Joe said.

"Something just doesn't seem right," Luke said to himself. "I'm going to look into this." He wandered over to the armory to see if he could tell what Mr. Ubsen was up to. He opened the door and not seeing anyone called, "Hello? Mr. Ubsen?" Not hearing a reply, Luke looked around the crates, over in the corner, where Joe had talked of rats, Luke noticed footprints leading to and facing the wall. The prints led to the wall, but none led away from it.

"That's odd," Luke said. He went to the wall and inspected it, running his hands over the wall to feel for a lever or switch. Feeling none, he gave it a push, like the secret door in the attic, and he heard a click and the door sprung toward him a few inches – enough to allow him to pull it open to reveal a hidden tunnel.

"This place is full of secret passageways," Luke said aloud.

"It sure is," said a voice at his left ear. The ever-calm Luke jumped in spite of himself and turned to see Ben looking into the tunnel in awe.

"Wow," he said.

"Wanna go explore?" Luke asked.

"Sure," Ben replied eagerly.

"Let me call Mom real quick," Luke said, pulling out his radio.

As Luke told Mom their location and plans, Ben went to the desk to check in some supplies that he was returning. "What?" he exclaimed.

Luke looked at him in surprise at his outburst.

Ben referred to the checklist on the clipboard. "Joe checked out the Flying Flambé' to Mr. Ubsen?"

"Yeah. Sounded fishy to me, too," Luke replied. "Joe said

Dad wanted it for special effects today."

"Dad would not ask for Joe's design to be used in this production," Ben explained. "What was Joe thinking?"

"He's preoccupied right now," Luke responded.

"And what is Mr. Ubsen trying to pull?" Ben asked fiercely. "Did you see which way he went?"

"Well, that's funny. I kept watching for him to come out of the armory, but I never saw him leave. I think maybe he took this tunnel," Luke said.

"Well, let's go then," Ben said switching on his flashlight and stepping into the tunnel.

The tunnel descended into a cavern, and Luke pointed to the ground and whispered, "I think he came this way."

A footprint of a work boot was embedded in the mud next to a cave puddle.

"I think you're right," Ben agreed. "Do you have any idea where this tunnel leads?" he asked.

Luke glanced at his GPS. "We're headed for the cave system and the Orpheum," Luke interpreted as they made their way through the dim tunnels.

Chapter 10   Paul's Salt

Meanwhile, the cast had gathered at the Orpheum, which Mom had turned into a cafeteria to serve the cast and crew sandwiches and salad.

"Come on kids – grab some lunch. So did you give my message to Orpheus?" she grinned.

"Yeah," said Logan. "Funny thing though, we never saw Euridice."

"Yeah – she's computer generated later," Mom laughed.

"Dori, come and eat – I brought a peanut butter and jelly sandwich just for you," Mom called to Dori.

"Okay, Mom, but can I eat and walk at the same time?" Dori asked.

"I guess that would be fine, but don't bother the cast and crew. They are eating a quick lunch, and then need to get back to work – it's a tight schedule today."

"Oh, I won't bother them. I just want to look at their shoes,"

Dori said as she wandered off.

Logan looked and Rachael and rolled his eyes, "Girls." He said.

"Dori does love cute shoes," Rachael agreed.

"Is she in the market for a pair of men's work boots?" Logan pointed to Dori, who was leaning down, examining the boots of a group of the crew who was standing in a circle, eating their sandwiches.

"Who knows," said Rachael, getting Dori's attention, and motioning for her to come to them. "Dori, what are you doing?"

"Looking for a spy," Dori whispered.

"And what does a spy look like?" Logan whispered back.

"I don't know," Dori whispered.

How will you know when you find him then?" asked Logan, "That is if it's a him?"

"He wears work boots that have a black moon on the toe," she said.

"Hmmm," said Logan. "Right or left?"

Dori looked at her own feet, compared her hands and said, "Left. It was his left boot," she said with a nod of her head. "Will you help me look?'

"Well, Dori, it's not really polite to go around and examine people's shoes," Rachael said hesitantly.

"Here, follow my lead," said Logan, as he went over to some of the guys from the camera crew, "Awesome action today – so

I'm curious. Do you use a special lens or setting when video recording in a cave?" As Logan and Rachael listened to their response, Dori casually looked at the work boots of the camera crew. She shook her head slightly to Rachael, who wrapped up the conversation by saying, "Thank you so much for explaining that. We better not bother you anymore. Thanks. Bye," she said, moving on to another group of crewmembers.

They had made their way around the Orpheum before most of the cast and crew headed back to the cavern for more movie-making, but Dori had not found her suspect.

"What secret is this spy trying to steal anyway?" Logan questioned.

"The secret to Joe's new design, The Flying Flambé." Dori explained.

"How do you know that?" Rachael asked.

"He was east dropping at the barn dance," Dori said importantly.

"East dropping?" Logan asked.

"I think you mean eavesdropping," Rachael explained as Logan smirked.

"Joe said that his fireworks had a secret ingredient," Dori said.

"Oh yeah? What's that?" Logan asked

"Paul's Salt," Dori said with intrigue while Rachael and Logan looked at each other in confusion.

"Hey come on, let's get back to the cavern, and see what happens next," said Logan. He gave a quick wave to Mom across the Orpheum, and pointed to the cave tunnel, with an eager questioning look.

She smiled and gave them the okay sign, as they scurried after the crew to the set location deep in the heart of the earth.

Chapter 11   Where There's Smoke There's Fire

The clouds gathered outside the abbey creating a gray canopy that darkened Joe's lab slowly and sinisterly. Joe sat for a moment staring at the smoky contents of a beaker. The chemicals he had poured into the beaker reacted to produce a cloud of swirling vapor.

"I've produced smoke without fire – evidence without energy. The old saying, 'Where there's smoke, there's fire,' has been disproved. Usually smoke indicates fire; it is the messenger that spreads the word of the ferocity of the fire. In darkness you can't see smoke, but the fire tells its own tale. Pyrotechnicians depend on darkness to magnify their displays. Perhaps I have just discovered the secret to daytime displays that are filled with colorful smoke and thunderous excitement," he mused, but he was strangely unexcited about this discovery.

"Smoke can tell a story, too – or reveal one," Joe argued with himself. "I feel like I am surrounded by a cloud of smoke, unable to get my bearings – unable to see things as they really are. A force of which I am unaware has blinded me. I'm surrounded by a silhouette of something sinister, and yet my proximity to it keeps me from seeing what it is."

"Why do I disappoint Dad? Why is Mr. Ubsen promoted, while I am removed from my position? Why does Dad want my masterpiece? Why does he put my creation into the hands of someone like Mr. Ubsen?"

It didn't make sense for Dad to ask for the Flying Flambé'. If Joe hadn't felt so badly about the botched special effect, perhaps he would have realized it didn't line up. He'd been so focused on his own accomplishments lately, that he didn't see other things clearly.

Suddenly a clap of thunder resounded and for an instant Joe was awakened from his stupor as the light of truth flashed with momentarily revelation. Like lightening at midnight exposes a hidden world for just a moment, before erasing it in blackness, Joe saw the truth.

"Dad didn't take my design." Immediately darkness returned, but now Joe had a vision to hold on to. In the midst of swirling smoke, he had an anchor of hope. In the midst of the darkness he had a shining beacon that could lead him through the storm.

"I'd better go check in with Dad and see what is going on," but he quickly second-guessed himself. "No, Dad isn't very happy with me right now. Maybe I should keep a low profile. Maybe I can check it out without being seen."

He remembered his old tunnel system. Joe hurried from his lab just as the clouds poured down water and the skies resounded with thunder as arrows flashed back and forth.

Joe pulled back beneath the roof of the covered walkway that connected the classrooms. He followed under the canopy to the library and like a bird flitters easily to its nest through the boughs and branches, Joe wove his way through the great high shelves of books to the darkened corner with the purple book with gold letters. He grasped the spine, the shelf swung open and Joe stepped into the darkened corridor.

He began to count as he stepped confidently into the dark, and when he reached 25, he stopped and felt the wall of the cave. His hands searched for a ledge, but he felt only a flat wall, roughened by erosion. "Where is it? It has to be here," he reasoned. "Oh, yeah," he grinned. "I was not so tall back then, and he dropped to his knees to make himself the approximate height of his first grade years. He still could not locate the hiding spot, and as his thoughts swirled, the answer was revealed. Joe retraced his steps in the dark to the cave entrance, turned and took smaller steps, like those of a seven-year-old boy. When he reached 25 again, he felt the wall and was relieved to feel the ledge – once way above his head, but now at shoulder height.

He removed a stone, and sighed in relief as he felt the handle of the metal box he had hidden so many years before. He pulled it out, brushed it off, imagining how the vibrant images of the colorful racing cars must have faded through the years of cave dwelling. He flipped down the latch of the old tin lunch box, opened the lid, felt inside, and pulled out an object that fit into the palm of his hand like a familiar tool. As he squeezed the trigger a weak glow lit up the cave, and Joe grinned to see the contents of his old lunch box for a moment. He flipped the lid closed and strode purposefully down the passageway, lunch box in one hand, and flashlight in the other. Every few steps he squeezed the handle of the machine, which turned the gears and created an electrical flow that lit the bulb and produced a small temporary stream of light.

As Joe made his way through the familiar tunnel, his way alternately lit by momentary bursts of energy from the dynamo flashlight, and then obscured by blackest night, his thoughts followed the same patterns of light and dark. He held onto the light. "Dad wouldn't take my design," but the dark whispered, "Someone did." "Dad wouldn't take my design," "But Mr. Ubsen did," "Dad wouldn't take my design," "Jake Ubsen has your design. Why does he want it? What will he do with it? It's gone forever. Now you'll never win the national contest."

"Dad wouldn't take my design. . . Dad wouldn't. . . Dad. . . Dad. . . Dad will know what to do." Suddenly Joe had a longing for his father like he hadn't felt for years. Joe had followed his father's example and excelled in everything. He had striven to be strong and confidant like his father, but in his quest for excellence and to prove his competence to his father, to win his approval, he had somehow distanced himself from the one thing he longed for most – his father.

He suddenly felt like a little boy, whose exhilaration of riding his bicycle for the first time was suddenly extinguished by a hidden bump in the road that twisted the tire, and wrenched the handlebars from his inexperienced hands, landing all in a heap on the road, the bruised and bleeding boy left to cling and cry in the strong arms of his indestructible father.

That brief feeling that flashed with brilliance momentarily was extinguished by Joe's scoffing, "Humph – well, I'm almost a man now, and I need to solve this myself. I got myself into this mess, and I need to get myself out of it. This tunnel will lead me to the set, and I'll confront Mr. Ubsen and find out what is going on."

Chapter 12   The Pride of Thunder

Rachael, Logan and Dori made their way to the set, which was in an area of the cave where several tunnels converged into a large open cavern that provided several backdrops for making great cave scenes. The expert lighting crew could vary the light from dark and creepy to firelight friendly, and one side of the cavern provided an awesome backdrop of boulders, crevasses, stalagmites and shadowy effects that would add intrigue and mystery to the movie they were creating.

Rachael and Dori took a seat on a rock ledge, while Logan went from one technician to another. He knew that in order to be a welcome guest on this set, he would have to be quiet and stay out of the way. No one could be quiet as noisily as Logan could. His delight was declared in his expressive countenance. His amazement was announced by the awe shouted silently from every atom of his being. He exploded with excitement and exuded enthusiasm as he silently observed.

His attitude was appealing, and the technicians took pleasure in inviting him to have a closer look. Rachael saw the cameraman offer Logan a look at the video display. Next time she looked, the lighting tech was allowing Logan to help move and station the light tripods. Then she saw him touching up the makeup lines on Poseidon's face with the make-up artist. After that he was distributing props. Dori wanted to go to Logan and participate in the action, but Rachael distracted her by descriptively explaining from afar what Logan was learning hands-on.

"Places everyone," their father announced.

"Oh, goody," Dori exclaimed. "It's Poseidon and Brontes again."

"Yes, the story continues with an altercation between Poseidon and Zeus. Poseidon is the mythical ruler of the earth and sea, and Zeus is his brother, the ruler of the sky."

The cameraman's assistant held up the clapperboard, that read, 'Poseidon's Pride, Scene 3, Take 1'.

"Action," Dad said authoritatively.

Brontes struck the final blow on the completed glowing prongs of the trident and plunged it into a wooden pail of water. The glow was darkened by the hissing of the water as a cloud of smoke rose from the pail, Brontes raised the steaming trident from the water and held it up for Poseidon's inspection.

Poseidon eagerly grasped the trident and held it high, and as he held it up, it began to glow and thunder rumbled from its prongs.

"You dare to thunder?" a voice rumbled from the darkness. "I am the ruler of the thunder. I will not share my glory with another." A lightening bolt shot at the feet of Poseidon, which was swallowed in the shimmering pool of water that surrounded Poseidon.

"You are the ruler of the air, but I am the ruler of the sea and earth," Poseidon declared, as he pointed his trident to the ground and caused an invisible and non-existent slight earthquake tremor, cuing the actors to stagger as though losing their balance.

Dori put her hand over her mouth to stifle a giggle.

"Cut," called their father, and immediately the characters relaxed into normal people wearing costumes. Rachael looked up to see Ben and Luke coming toward her as they emerged from one of the tunnels that opened into the large cavern.

Dori giggled aloud now, "Ben did you see them staggering around?"

"Yeah. That is funny looking. When they add the special effects and computer generated graphics later it will look real though."

"Where did you guys come from?" Logan asked as he loped up to the group.

"We found a new tunnel that leads here from the armory,"

Ben replied.

"Yeah – we think we're following Mr. Ubsen – have you seen him?" Luke asked.

"He was gone earlier, but I think he's getting ready for the next scene, when they add in some special effects," said Logan, who had learned a lot from the crew.

"Dori, where are you going?" Rachael asked, looking after the girl who was wandering away with an intent look.

"I'll be right back. I'm looking for the moon," she called back in a loud whisper.

Rachael shrugged her shoulders and turned back to the boys. "Why are you following Mr. Ubsen?" she quizzed.

"There is something strange going on," Luke said.

"What?" Logan asked eagerly.

"Well, we don't know yet, but it's something mysterious," said Luke.

"Kind of suspicious," Ben added.

"Oooh," said Logan with a gleam of excitement in his eye. "Tell us all about it."

"Well, Mr. Ubsen told Joe that Dad wanted his Flying Flambé', and Joe gave it to him" Ben explained.

"That doesn't make sense," Rachael wrinkled her brow reflectively.

"Well, just ask Dad," said Logan. "He's right over there," he pointed to their father in consultation with some of the crew.

"He's busy, and we don't want it to look like we're questioning his decisions," Ben cautioned.

"You're right," said Luke. "We might be able to find out some more info before we have to bother Dad."

"Like what?" asked Logan, pulling a small notepad from his pocket. "I'll take notes. Mr. Ubsen has the Flying Flambé'."

"Dori saw someone eavesdropping while Joe talked about his secret ingredient," Rachael added.

"Yeah. What did she call it?" Logan asked.

"Paul's salt," Rachael said.

"She must have meant saltpetre. That's gun powder," Luke said.

"The spy has a crescent-shaped mark on their boot," Logan said.

"Someone has been using a secret tunnel from the armory," Ben added.

"Joe's special effects have been sabotaged," Logan added.

"Well, we don't know they've been sabotaged," Ben corrected.

"Well, Joe's stuff always works, and now suddenly it doesn't," Logan defended his statement.

"What's different now?" asked Rachael.

"I'm not sure, except Mr. Ubsen seems to be a common denominator," said Luke.

"He does always seem to be around when something goes

wrong," Ben admitted.

"He's always lurking furtively," Logan said accusingly.

"Take 2," the cameraman's assistant called.

"Action," Dad called loudly, and Ben hushed everyone as they piled on the ledge. Rachael looked around for Dori, but didn't see her.

Poseidon repeated his last line, '... ruler of the sea and earth."

"My power is greater," shouted Zeus.

"No more than the air is greater than the sea," Poseidon gushed like the sound of many waters. "Your conceit has blinded you to the truth, my brother,"

A lightening bolt thundered from his hand, "How so?" demanded Zeus.

"I can survive in air or sea, but you, as ruler of the sky, depend on air."

Zeus flashed his lightening.

"We are both powerful in our own realm. Do not allow your pride to darken your realm," Poseidon said.

"I am the ruler of thunder and lightening. I can produce darkness and light," Zeus retorted.

"Yes, but the power of your lightening is brief and fleeting, and always accompanied by storm and cloud. But watch this. I can cause the earth to tremble," and they fell silent for the effect. "I can cause the sea to writhe."

"And together we rule the world of mortal men," Zeus replied powerfully.

"And so brother, let us say farewell in peace, each of us to rule well and justly."

"Very well," said Zeus. "You will see me in the storm," he said as in a great show of thunder and lightening, he faded.

"Cut," shouted Mr. Livingstone. "I want to set up and shoot this from a different angle, and this time we will set off the exit explosion. Poseidon will disappear as an artesian well springs up, and his feet and his garments become the water – blue at the bottom, gradually becoming white as he disappears and the bubbling fountain remains. We'll generate the fountain later as a computer graphic, but we'll need to record for a full minute after the explosion."

"Whoa – cool," breathed Logan.

Chapter 13 Take Cover!

The tunnel converged with the same cavern where the crew was working. Joe watched the last scene and when his father yelled cut, he approached Mr. Ubsen and said, "Mr. Ubsen, may I have a word with you?"

"Beat it kid. I have important work to do," Mr. Ubsen replied.

"Mr. Ubsen, I'd like to ask what you intend to do with the Flying Flambé'" Joe asked.

"The what?"

"The fireworks that you got from me today."

"Don't know what you're talking about. I've been here all day, doing the work of two people," Mr. Ubsen grunted as he busied himself with explosives for the next scene.

"I don't know what you're up to, but it will never work. That formula has already been entered in the national festival as my design. You won't get away with entering it yourself."

Mr. Ubsen straightened up and laughed at Joe. "That amateur festival? The prize money is peanuts compared to," he stopped abruptly. "Go away and play with your firecrackers. This is no place for a novice."

Joe was angry, but he realized there was more at stake than his ego. He said, "You leave me no choice but to speak to my father."

As Joe turned to go to his father, Mr. Ubsen fidgeted and quickly replied, "Okay, okay, okay. I'll talk to you, but just wait until after this scene. I have to finish this and then I'll tell you everything you want to know."

"All right," Joe said.

"Just wait for me down this tunnel," Jake pointed down a darkened narrow passageway. I'll come get you when I'm finished."

"Why there? Why can't I stay here and watch the shoot?"

Um—you'll uh—make me nervous if you watch. Just do me a favor and stay out of the way."

"Okay," Joe shrugged and headed down the tunnel. He sat on a boulder and thought about what he would say to Mr. Ubsen, who was definitely lying. "Why? What did he have going on? And if he didn't want the Flying Flambé' for the festival, then what was his interest in it?"

Joe paused in an alcove where he could watch unseen. He loved the action on a movie set, and was especially interested in this scene where Poseidon and Zeus exited in a great display of thundering and smoke with small explosive charges to replicate lightening. A small amount of explosive could produce much flashing brilliance, much like the effect of a sparkler in the hand of a child on a dark Fourth of July evening.

These effects were easy and commonplace, but Joe still enjoyed watching the process. Joe saw Mr. Ubsen take a blasting cap from his pocket, and wondered, "What Mr. Ubsen was doing with a blasting cap?" This scene didn't call for blasting caps. No safety protocol had been established, and the set should be cleared of non-authorized personnel if he planned to set off an actual explosion.

Joe paused for a moment in indecision. "I wish I'd been at the production meeting this morning. Maybe I missed a major change in the production schedule," he reflected. "Either way, I need to check into this. The safety of the crew is more important than me looking stupid, or getting in trouble," he decided.

He heard his dad's voice echo through the caverns, "Action," and thought, "It won't be long now and I'll have the answers I want."

While Joe walked toward the cavern and the movie set, he noticed enough dynamite to explode through the wall of the cave and cause a cave-in. Miners used these types of explosives in mining to clear out an area of a mine; the dynamite was connected to the blasting cap, which led to a detonator at the feet of Jake Ubsen, whose hand was poised to push the handle to detonate the blast.

Poseidon repeated his last line and Mr. Livingstone gave Mr. Ubsen the cue to set off the minor explosive charge for the special effect.

Suddenly Joe shouted, "Cut. Take Cover," as he raced to stop Mr. Ubsen. Mr. Ubsen turned his head to the sound of Joe's voice and raised his eyes in surprise as he pushed down the handle, and dove for cover. An enormous flash of light exploded in Joe's face, singeing his hair, and blackening his face.

The blast threw him backward just as boulders shuddered and rocks showered all over and around him. A rock hit Joe's forehead; he was knocked to the ground, stunned by the blow, but rolled to the edge of the tunnel to take cover under a rock outcropping just as the thundering rocks began to roll. Thick dust rose, and Joe covered his nose with his shirt collar to protect his lungs from the thick dusty air.

Rachael was relieved to see Dori slide next to her as she heard an urgent voice call 'Cut! Take Cover!' she glimpsed her Dad's concerned look just before he rushed to one of the cameramen, tackled him, and pushed him back from the camera just as a thunderous explosion blasted, and a shower of rocks came crashing into the tripod.

"Everyone, cover your face with your sleeve, and follow Hank's blue light," shouted Mr. Livingstone as he helped direct everyone to safety. He quickly turned to Ben and said, "Ben, get the kids out." He called after Hank, "Take a head count as soon as you get out and compare it to your roster." He helped the cameraman, who was lying stunned on the floor, to his feet, and checked him for injuries. "Only a little dirt and dust," he said.

Chapter 14 Blinded by the Light

As darkness covered him like the cloud of dust, Joe staggered to his feet. He heard nothing except tumbling rocks. Spots and flashes of light appeared before him, and he rubbed his eyes, but could see nothing else. He heard no screams or cries of fright, no shouting from the cavern.

"I'm trapped in the tunnel, blocked by yards of fallen rock. I can't see or hear the others, so I can't leave the cave from that direction." He felt warm liquid streaming down his face, and pulled a handkerchief from his pocket and applied pressure to the wound. He was dizzy and disoriented.

The oozing wound stopped wetting the handkerchief, so he tied it around his head. No one but the Livingstone boys still carried handkerchiefs in their pockets these days. Mom said a well-mannered man would always have a handkerchief in his pocket. Mom was smart that way, and Joe pledged to himself that after today, he would never go anywhere without a handkerchief in his pocket.

He turned and felt his way, stumbling over rocks that were strewn over the pathway. He was forced to get on his hands and knees and crawl over the rocks. As he groped, his hands touched a square metal object, and he sat down in relief and opened the lid. As his hands closed around the familiar flashlight, it was like shaking hands with an old friend. Joe squeezed the trigger in eager anticipation of the light, as if it were a welcome cool drink on a hot day, but his old friend failed him. "The bulb must be broken," he said in disappointment, as he set the flashlight aside.

"Oh, well – plan B." He fumbled in the box until his fingers closed around a cylindrical object, and an accompanying rectangular box. He slid open the box, removed a thin stick, struck it against the box, and prepared to light the wick of the candle. He heard the familiar scrape and burst of flame, but didn't see the light. He started to strike it again, but as he brought the match tip near the box, it burned his finger. In confusion he lit three more matches, listened to them crackle with light, smelled the burning phosphorus, and felt the invisible flame burn his skin before he finally admitted incredulously to himself, "I can't see. I'm blind."

His fingers frantically sorted through the contents of his old lunchbox as he took inventory of his few supplies. He grinned as his fingers recognized the MRE army rations he'd put in as a boy. "At least I won't starve for a day or two," he chuckled sarcastically. "Good thing, too, because no one knows I'm here," Joe winced as he realized he'd broken the first rule of spelunking – never enter a cave alone without telling someone of your plans. Joe realized he'd been ignoring a lot of rules lately.

"Well, at least I can call them with my radio," Joe felt in his pocket for the radio, and realized with a sinking feeling in his stomach that he had removed it, set it on his workbench, and rushed off without it.

"At some point they will realize I'm missing – at least by dinner time today. They will form a search party and come after me. The kids know about the library tunnel, so they'll search it at some point. I could wait here for hours, or make my way through the dark on my own. I think I'll opt for that," Joe decided as he gingerly felt the wound on his head.

He felt through his box, and was reassured to find other caving supplies he had stored in the box years before. He took out a stick of chalk, and made an arrow on the wall of the cave pointing the direction he was headed, and added his initials below it.

His fingers closed around a cylindrical object, and he grinned as he unfolded it and tapped it on the ground. It was the walking stick that his great-uncle had given him; it was the type of cane that was used by blind persons to tap the ground while they walked to tell them what was in their path. He'd had fun pretending he was a blind boy in the caves, and had gotten pretty good at feeling his way along the cave with his eyes closed, but this darkness was thick and lonely, and much different than just closing your eyes in the dark at night. He unfolded the walking stick and tapped the ground slowly, and retraced his steps back through the tunnel toward the library.

For Joe, the slow pace was excruciating. He tapped with the cane for a few paces, made an arrow on the cave wall, and then went a few more paces. He was confidant that he could find his way back to the library tunnel. There were only a few places the cave branched off into unexplored trails, so if he could just be sure to stay in the main tunnel, he would be at the library soon enough, and he could get some medical attention for his eyes, and the cut on his forehead. He rubbed his eyes, and struck another match to see if his sight had returned, but the darkness still covered him like a thick cloak that threatened to smother him if he didn't fight it.

*

Hank called each name of the crew to make sure everyone who had been in the cave was accounted for.

Dori pulled on Rachael's sleeve, but Rachael hushed her.

"Dori, just wait until it calms down," Rachael instructed.

"But I found the moon," Dori said.

"Great – but just wait a minute," Rachael said.

Dori turned to Ben, "Ben, I know who the spy is."

"All right, Dori, but we can't do anything right now," Ben explained.

Logan, was reliving the excitement of the cave-in, "Man, did you see that cloud of smoke?

"I never thought I'd get another breath of fresh air," Rachael said.

"Did you see Dad save the cameraman?" Luke asked.

"Yeah, that was lucky. If Dad hadn't yelled 'Cut,' and 'Take Cover!', when he did, somebody could have gotten hurt," Ben said.

"Dad didn't yell 'Cut!'," Dori said.

"Of course he did, Dori," Rachael explained. "Only the director can yell cut."

"That wasn't Dad," Dori said insistently.

"Well, if it wasn't Dad, who was it?" Luke asked curiously.

"Well, it sounded like Joe," Dori said.

"It couldn't have been Joe. He was at his lab when we left there," Ben said, and Luke nodded in agreement.

Hank shouted, "Has anyone seen Jake?"

"Who is Jake?" Dori asked.

"That's Mr. Ubsen," Ben explained.

"Yeah. I saw him. He grabbed a box and then he went down

a tunnel," said the cameraman, who had a different vantage point from the ground were he had been sprawled after the cave-in.

"Why didn't he come here with everybody else?" Hank asked the cameraman, who just shrugged.

Dori pulled Rachael's arm.

"What is it, Dori?" Rachael asked in frustration.

"It's about Mr. Ubsen." Dori said.

"What about Mr. Ubsen?" Rachael asked.

"He's the spy," Dori whispered.

"What?" Rachael demanded in surprise.

"He has the moon on his boot," Dori said loud enough for all the kids to hear.

"Okay, everybody, we need to have a meeting," Luke said. "Logan, tell Mr. Hank that we're all accounted for, and we're heading for the library."

Luke led the way up the mountain and along the path to the Abbey. No one wanted to go back into the caverns now, and they needed the sunlight and fresh air to clear their lungs. As they came to the stable, Ben stopped abruptly and said, "Shhh!"

Luke followed the direction he saw Ben staring and saw Mr. Ubsen appear from a storm cellar, built into the hillside. In years past it had been used for storage to keep milk chilled and to store the canned goods, and to keep things fresh. Built into the ground, and with a spring running through it, it was an ideal storage place. The kids crouched behind a feeding trough and watched as Mr. Ubsen furtively looked around and walked quickly through the barnyard. He carried an old army bag over one shoulder, and a medium size box carefully tucked under one arm.

"Looks like he's taking off," Ben said.

"In a hurry," said Rachael.

"With Joe's Flying Flambé'," Luke said.

"Should we try to stop him?" asked Logan, ready for action.

"Nah," said Ben. "We can't detain him. He is free to go wherever he wants. Let's go figure this out." He headed for the storm cellar, poked his head inside the small building, and saw the tunnel door that Mr. Ubsen must have left open in his haste.

"Come on," Logan yelled, going through the doorway. It was a short tunnel that came out in the courtyard of the abbey. As they emerged from the tunnel, Logan tripped and sprawled on the ground. Luke, who was right behind him, had to scramble, and vault over him to make sure he didn't fall on top of him, and Ben stopped short, causing Dori and Rachael to barrel into him.

Logan rolled to his knees to examine what had tripped him. He saw a large cylindrical object imbedded in the ground, and pushed on it to roll it from the ground.

"Hey, look. It's part of a statue," he said.

Dori bent down and traced the letters etched on a banner that wrapped around the flowing rock garment of the statue. "Seph," she read. "I wonder what poor Seph looked like?" she said, as she caressed his lonely torso, missing his head and chest.

"Here's the pedestal where the poor guy belongs," Rachael said, pointing to a concrete pedestal in the Roman Doric style, that stood like a lonely column in the abbey courtyard.

"Wonder what knocked the poor fellow from his pedestal?" Luke pondered.

"Probably the same thing that brings most down," Ben replied.

"What's that?" Logan asked.

"Pride and arrogance," Ben answered. "Come on," he said as he led the way to the library.

Perched on one of the lower rungs of a library ladder, Luke looked like Rodin's 'The Thinker' on his pedestal. Logan climbed past him and stood on one foot on an upper rung, reaching up to grasp a wooden spindle in the railing on the next level. He looked like a sailor hanging from the mast, looking ahead for stormy seas.

Rachael and Dori arranged themselves at the heavy old oak tables in the study area, and Ben paced back and forth with his hands in his pockets, and with his ball cap tilted sideways.

"Okay," said Luke, "What do we know so far?"

Logan read from his notes: "Mr. Ubsen has the Flying Flambé'. Dori saw someone with a crescent shaped mark on his boot.

"Mr. Ubsen," Dori muttered.

"Someone was using the tunnel from the armory," Logan continued.

"Mr. Ubsen," said Luke.

"Joe's special effects were sabotaged," Logan read.

"Well, today's special effects were certainly sabotaged," said Ben. "And Joe wasn't in charge."

"Mr. Ubsen was," Rachael said.

"Mr. Ubsen either intentionally or accidentally through neglect or ignorance caused the cave-in today," said Ben.

"And now he's run off," said Logan.

"Someone besides Dad yelled cut before the cave-in," Dori added.

"Jake Ubsen is the common denominator," Luke said.

"I told you he was a spy," Dori said. "Joe has a secret ingredient in his Flying Flambé', and someone's trying to steal it."

"Jake Ubsen," repeated Luke.

"What did you say?" Ben said.

"Mr. Ubsen," repeated Luke.

"No. You said -- ,"

"Jake Ubsen," Luke said quickly.

"That's it," Ben said.

"What?" asked Logan

"A connection we've overlooked," Ben said.

"What?" they all said together.

"Right before we came home, the program director introduced us to a man who wanted to buy Joe's Flying Flambé'. He offered Joe a lot of money for it," Ben explained.

"So what's that got to do with Mr. Ubsen?" Logan asked confused.

"The man's name was Mr. Jacobson," Ben said.

They all looked at him blankly with a questioning look.

"Jake Ubsen – Jacobson!" Ben said.

Their mouths dropped open in understanding.

Maybe Jake Ubsen is really Mr. Jacobson, a relative to Mr. Jacobson, working for Colossal Creations. Maybe he stole the Flying Flambé' for Mr. Jacobson.

"That's a serious allegation," said Luke.

"It is, and we shouldn't repeat it without checking it out, but we can certainly look into it," Rachael said.

"Yes, but somehow Joe is connected to this," Ben said.

"Yeah," Luke agreed.

"I told you Joe was the one who yelled cut," Dori said.

"Joe is working in his lab, Dori. It couldn't have been him," Ben explained.

"Why don't we get Joe to help us," Rachael suggested. "If it involves him, he can help us solve it."

"Good idea. I'll go get him," Logan jumped to the floor, and ran out the door toward Joe's lab. A minute later he burst through the door and panted, "He's not in his lab. And here's his radio."

They all fell quiet as they realized the truth. Joe must have been in the tunnel where the cave-in occurred. The children stared at each other for a moment before they jumped to their feet.

"I'll call Dad," Ben said seriously as he drew his radio from his pocket, and as he began to explain the situation, Luke and Logan raced to the armory and grabbed some spelunking gear. When they got back to the library, Ben was ready to take charge of the eager crew.

Chapter 15   Vertigo

Darkness is a bottomless pit with no frame of reference. What is right or left, under or over, near or far? Is the world spinning around? Where are the familiar landmarks that my eyes use for clues to help me keep my balance, to give me direction, to help me know where I am in relation to the big wide world around me?

Where in the world am I in the dark? It could be China or the moon, but with no fixed point to guide me, I don't even know where I am.

A cloudy sky guides no sailor. I am a ship without a sextant, a plane without a pilot, a boat without an oar, adrift in a sea. No, it's worse than that. I am a boat without an oar, adrift in an undiscovered ocean, on a cloudy night during the new moon, without a star in the sky, in the middle of a whirlpool. I'm going in dizzying circles, around and around, getting ready to be sucked into a bottomless pit of darkness."

Joe stumbled as his thoughts created a vertigo which brought him to his knees. He lowered himself to the floor and spread out with his back on the cool floor of the cave. In the darkness Joe felt himself spinning on a merry-go-round, the centrifugal force weighing him down.

He felt like he was on a spinning wheel, and he was the arrow that a giant kept flicking with his finger, just to watch it spin and spin. As soon as it slowed, he flicked again and Joe went spinning again. His chest was pinned to the cave floor with a weight like a concrete block on his chest, but he was spinning around and around and around.

Joe willed himself to make the spinning stop. Think of the cool cave floor, not the evil giant. As he swung to a stop, he tried to sit up, but now the dark world was spinning around him. Or was he falling? Maybe he was in a bottomless pit with the walls rushing past, surrounded by darkness, but hurtling through space, confined in a black hole where all time stops and only thoughts rush.

I'm going to lose myself in this black hole of nothingness if I don't control my thoughts," Joe realized. "I'm not in a black hole. I'm not falling. I'm sitting here in a cave with my eyes closed. It's just dark, but I can imagine what it looks like."

As Joe began to envision his dark world in his mind, he slowly turned the lights on in his imagination. He used the sounds of the cave to distract him from the dark fear that threatened to envelope him. He heard water plopping down from the stalactites, which clung tightly to the cave ceiling. Each droplet of water left a microscopic residue of limestone from calcium carbonate, which over many years allowed the stalactite to grow toward the cave floor, a worthy endeavor, but now Joe used the droplets to learn about his surroundings.

Occasionally he heard a scurrying sound of some similarly blind cave creature escaping what? Oh, me. Several times he felt a large creature swish past his shoulder. It must be a bat, but the sound of the swooshing of displaced air made it seem to be a large and gigantic bat. "My mind is playing tricks," Joe thought. "This tunnel feels like a cavern to me, and yet it is a small tunnel," he said aloud.

"That's odd," he said, as his voice echoed. He shouted, and his voice reverberated. In the blindness you must rely on your other senses: hearing, smell, taste, touch. So Joe held out his hands to feel the tunnel walls. He felt the cave wall, wet with dampness on his left, but no wall on his right, as he groped, taking several steps and feeling strangely vulnerable and alone in the emptiness.

"I will have to find other ways to see my surroundings." He waved his cane around, but it connected with only thin air. He stooped to the ground and grabbed a handful of small pebbles and threw it blindly in the air, listening as it quietly filtered through the air and rained at his feet.

Joe realized with a strange terror, that he was in a new area of the cave. This unfamiliar and unexplored region could have drop-offs, or deep pools of water, or dead-end tunnels. If he was to safely navigate this cavern, he needed more information, but how was he to get information in the dark?

"I am going to have to rely on feedback from my surroundings. I must get the cave to tell me what I want to know. He stooped again and found several pebbles. He threw one toward the ceiling, but not directly overhead, since as Isaac Newton had proved with his law of gravity: what goes up must come down, and Joe didn't need any more injuries.

The pebble hit the cave floor. It had fallen to earth, but had not hit the ceiling. He threw another pebble higher. It too, hit the floor without sending back a signal that it had ever touched the cave ceiling. He threw pebbles toward the walls and mapped out in his mind the approximate dimensions of the cavern. It was a very large cavern, not quite as large as the Orpheum, but huge nonetheless.

Joe spent some time throwing out his rock signals to paint a picture of his surroundings. Another large winged creature flew past and Joe wondered what kind of bat this was. Like a bat, Joe was relying on echolocation, dependent on signals to tell him about his world. He recalled what he had learned of bats in his science classes, and especially of a colorful book back in the abbey library where he had first discovered the delightful creature back in first grade.

A bat sends out signals and waits for the sound waves to bounce off of something. It uses those return signals to tell him about his surroundings. It is like sonar the navy uses underwater to see what is in the pathway of a submarine. It is like a Doppler effect used by weathermen – they send out a signal, and based on the bounced back signals, create a picture of the impending storm.

"I wonder what is wrong with my radar," Joe mused. "Why could I not see this impending storm approaching? I'm in a big mess now, because I was blind to the signals."

Joe continued to rest and reflect on the principles of echolocation. He recalled a school program conducted by a weatherman who told of a phenomenon called the horseshoe effect. This anomaly was seen during converging storm systems. When the Doppler signals were sent out, an open horseshoe pattern came back, indicating strong activity on the left and right, but less activity ahead, in the curve of the horseshoe.

To pilots, it appeared that the path ahead, between the two storms was clear, but a plane disastrously entering that pattern would find itself in the midst of a ferocious storm. Evidently the huge storm ahead absorbed the signals, and although the storms on either side sent back accurate readings, it created a false impression of clear skies straight ahead. The echo feedback was correct, but the interpretation of the data was not correct. Now, when weathermen see a horseshoe pattern, they are alerted to a major storm system behind the two converging systems.

"I have been headed for this storm for some time, but I have completely misinterpreted the data. Something has skewed my ability to assess the data, and it is even more important that I learn the answer now that I am blind to normal stimuli," Joe reflected.

Joe rose to his feet again, with renewed determination to get his bearings and to find his way from this world of darkness. Now some might wonder why Joe didn't just retrace his steps to where the tunnel forked and go down the right path.

But, as Joe had discovered, he was trapped in a world of faulty reasoning, and didn't make the obvious and wise choice. He continued his way on a path of uncertainty and dubious outcome.

He grabbed a pocketful of pebbles and began to throw them. He heard the plunk of a pebble landing in a puddle, and edged nearer. He threw several pebbles before he discovered it was a pool at least ten feet across before a dry area of land was heard. He poked his cane into the water and could feel no bottom. It could be a bottomless pool, leading to an underground river. Joe shivered. Although it would normally be an adventure to scuba dive in that pool, and explore the source – it seemed a formidable foe in his present predicament.

As Joe stood in the center of the cavern surrounded by an ocean of darkness, waves of blackness washing over him in a tide of terror, Joe felt like he was drowning in darkness. The darkness was heavy. He could feel it. He was sinking beneath the black waves, and he held his breath to avoid breathing in the blackness. His lungs were bursting, but he was unwilling to breath the heavy blackness. It was suffocating him in a sea of silence. Down, down, down into the depths he was sinking, until he could wait no longer. He must breathe. He gasped, and filled his lungs with the darkness, and now it seemed to overtake him completely. Even his thoughts were invaded by the sea of darkness.

A wave of despair washed over him, and a dark thought trickled into his mind, and then another and another flowed through his brain, crashing into the coast of his mentality. A tidal wave of hopelessness came crashing with great force, and Joe staggered under the weight of the invisible, yet powerful assault.

He felt something swim past his shoulder in the sea of silence. "It's a shark," Joe thought in desperation as it circled around again and brushed into him. He frantically waved his arms to swim, and felt only air. Joe shook his head to clear his thoughts. "I must have gotten hit hard. I'm beginning to hallucinate." He told himself sternly, "I am not in an ocean. This is just a big empty room underground. I'm just in the dark.

There are no sharks, and nothing to be afraid of. Just then something brushed his shoulder, and he heard a whoosh of air, and a flapping sound.

"It's just a bat," he reassured himself. There will be many bats hanging from the ceiling. One has awakened, and flew past," he reasoned calmly.

A piercing sound rent the air. It was a repetitive screeching sound, and Joe could almost feel the sound waves rushing toward him. The screeches came closer as something was nearing Joe, and then swooped past him. The bat was using his screeches to locate Joe and it circled around emitting its horrific shrieks.

"It is using echolocation to locate me. He can't see either. He is just as frightened of me as I am of him. His sounds bounce off me to show him a reflection of what I am, and where I am, and how big I am."

"He has the advantage because he can learn a lot about me, but I can't see him. I can tell where he is, by the sound signals he sends out."

"Yeah, I can hear him coming, so I'll know when he's going to attack," Joe said aloud.

The shrieking sounds grew louder, and faster, and the huge bat landed on Joe, and wrapped his two large membranous forelimbs around him. Joe flung the beast off, and it swooped away.

Joe waited in silence for the bat to reappear, but it was eerily quiet. "He's toying with me. He's waiting, trying to make me think he's gone away, and then he's going to fly past and scratch me with a talon."

The huge bat swooped near Joe and sliced a gash on his cheek. As the blood trickled down his face, Joe said, "The only way I can protect myself is to learn his ways and hit him with my cane." He waited until he heard him fly closer, and said, "A little closer, and I'll have a good shot at you." Quickly Joe swung his cane just above his left shoulder, and felt a jarring force as his cane connected with a very large object that was flung through the air, but then flew away.

"I'll be okay unless he has a friend," Joe thought. "I'm not sure I can battle two." Suddenly Joe heard shrieks coming from both directions and waved his cane, as though trying to hit dueling piñatas.

"Oh, no. What if the whole cavern of bats swarms around me?" Joe said aloud, and suddenly, as though in answer to his summons, a multitude of shrieks filled the cavern, and he heard the hoard approaching.

"It's as if they are reading my mind, and listening to my commands. Their actions are a reflection of my words, and my fear. When I speak my fears, then they are reflected in his actions. They bounce off as sound waves, and then are interpreted and enacted," Joe realized. "Well, take this then," he shouted, "Be gone. Go back to your pit," he commanded.

Immediately the crashing wave of shrieking demons subsided, and their reverberating echoes told him they were fleeing.

"That's interesting," he thought. "Come back," he shouted, and their sounds grew louder, "Be gone," he shouted in fright, hoping it would work again, and the receding raucous sound revealed that it had.

"Unbelievable," he thought. "A host of beings who do as they are bid. Their actions mirrored my words. They were echoing my signal. They were responding to my sonar. They fed on my fear, but had to comply with my command. Wow. So, I need to be sure to say good things from now on. Things like, I am going to find my way out of this cavern."

Joe turned away from the water and wandered to a new area of the cavern. He found a wall and followed it until an opening appeared – a tunnel. Was this the tunnel that would take him back to the library? Joe decided to take the tunnel, so marking a large arrow on the wall, he started down the tunnel. He soon came to a fork in the tunnel, and by now he was very disoriented. He didn't know if this was even the same tunnel he had been in before, and if so had he come from the right or left fork? There was no way to know since he hadn't known it forked.

He retrieved a ball of string from his lunch box, and tied it to a rock. "I might have to explore both arms of this tunnel, but at least I can find my way back." Joe wandered, unrolling the string and making chalk signs on the wall, feeling his way blindly with his cane, until his careful tapping of the path abruptly gave way, and Joe stopped suddenly at the edge of a precipice.

Joe scrambled to back away from the gaping pit, but disoriented from the darkness, and dizzy from the blow to his head, as he turned and groped for something to hang onto, a large winged beings swooped past him, and he slipped, lost his footing, and rolled, bumped and banged, clutching and grabbing for something to stop his fall, until gravity stopped his descent with a final blow that completely darkened his world in unconsciousness.

Chapter 16 Convergence

"Dad is at the shoot site, and he has a crew working to remove the rubble on that end. He wants us to come in the back way to that tunnel, since we're familiar with the caves," Ben relayed the information with urgency. "Quick. We have to decide which tunnel will get us to that branch fastest."

"What about the armory tunnel you took this morning?" Logan asked.

"No. That tunnel comes out at the shoot site," Luke explained.

"What about the one Joe showed us the first day he was here – by the Orpheum?" Logan added.

"Yeah, that one leads to several tunnels and the Orpheum," Luke agreed.

"Hey wait," Ben said. "There is another tunnel Joe likes to use."

"Where's Dori?" Rachael asked suddenly.

Dori wandered away from the group, following the sound of tinkling crystals. The sound led her through a maze of library shelves to the end of a long row of books. Suddenly a piercing scream reverberated through the rows of shelves.

Now, a little girl's piercing scream can mean lots of things. It can equally say, "Oh a new doll," or "Ew, an ugly spider."

As Logan knew, it could mean, "Don't tickle me,"

As Luke knew, it could say, "I just saw a snake,"

As Ben knew, it could shout, "I just love candy."

As Rachael knew, being well acquainted with Dori's squeals, it could also mean, "I'm so excited that I can do nothing but make this shrill piercing sound – but that's okay, because you'll all come running, and figure it out soon enough."

They followed Ben's lead, and soon saw what had caused Dori's squeal – the open shelf, revealing the way into Joe's cave tunnel. They moved quickly through the tunnel using their flashlights to guide them. This section of the cave had many meandering tunnels. The first several they came to, Ben and Luke quickly by-passed, knowing them to be tunnels they had explored that morning while searching with Joe for bat guano. Luke's GPS came in handy as he discounted several other tunnels that branched away from the direction of the caverns he knew the set was in.

They came to a dead-end wall of the cave, with a tunnel going right, and one going left.

"Which way now?" Ben asked Luke.

"Hmmm," Luke thought, "The set is straight in front of us, through this wall, either tunnel could curve around to where the set is," he explained.

"Maybe we should split up," Logan suggested.

"It would be faster," Rachael agreed.

"Okay, Luke. You go with Rachael and Dori down this tunnel," Ben nodded left.

"Logan and I will go this way. Keep in touch with your radio," Ben said as he headed right.

The girls and Luke had not walked very far when Dori said, "Look," pointing to the wall.

"Chalk mark," Luke observed.

"It's an arrow pointing this way," said Rachael.

"What's this under the arrow?" Dori asked.

"I think it's Joe's initials," Luke said excitedly. "He always writes them connected and squiggly like that."

"He must be okay," Rachael breathed relieved.

"Assuming these are fresh marks," Luke said, pressing the button on his radio to tell Ben what they'd found.

"That's great. You guys keep following that tunnel. If we don't see something soon, we'll join you, but I just want to go a little further. Logan thinks he smells gunpowder," Ben radioed back.

"Yeah, well you can trust Logan's nose – at least where food is concerned," Luke chuckled. "But you can probably trust it here, too."

"I've been wondering. If this is Joe's mark, why didn't he go back the tunnel to the library?" Rachael asked.

"He must have missed his turn-off," said Dori, who occasionally served as back-seat driver, especially quick with instructions when someone missed a turn.

The radio crackled, "Hey Luke, come back to us. We need your help on this end. Let the girls keep going," Ben said.

Luke gave his backpack of caving gear to Rachael, and took off at a run down the tunnel. As he saw the flashlights of Logan and Ben, he picked up his pace, and sprinted the last few yards to them.

"What's up?" he panted.

"Cave-in," said Ben. "Dad's on the other side clearing, and we should do the same," he said seriously.

"Ben – I don't think Joe's here. I think he went the other way down the tunnel," Luke said.

"Yeah, but just in case, we should clear this," Ben said as he and Logan grunted to move the rocks and boulders.

Luke could hear Dad's crew tapping faintly from the other side, and didn't want to think of Joe trapped or crushed beneath the rocks. He preferred to think of him making his way down the tunnel the girls were exploring – the tunnel he wanted to explore. He kicked at a rock in frustration, and then looked down and said, "Ben, look!"

At his feet were several burnt matches. Logan stooped down, picked one up, and put it to his nose. "It still has the smell of sulfur on it," he said excitedly. Let's look for more clues."

"We've got to get Joe out," Ben said frantically moving stones. "Come on, you guys. Help me."

Luke put his hand on Ben's shoulder, swung him around, and shook him gently. "Ben, it's going to be okay, but just think -- Joe might have lit these matches after the explosion."

"Or some crew member could have been sneaking a smoke," Ben said.

"Hey, what's this?" Logan cried, picking up an object from the ground. He squeezed the handle. "Cool. A flashlight that doesn't use batteries."

"Let me see that," Ben said. "I think I've seen this before – a long long time ago." He gently brushed his hand over the see-through plastic casing. "Hey, here's a mark," he said pointing to faded initials marked on the side.

"J.L. It must be Joe's," said Luke.

"Pretty messy writing," said Logan.

"He probably wrote it when he was six or seven. He told me he had hidden a lunch box in the cave," Ben said slowly.

"Why would he leave a perfectly good flashlight behind," said Logan.

Ben looked at the pile of rocks and increased his speed as he frantically removed one boulder at a time.

Logan and Luke turned away from Ben as they looked for more clues on the ground.

"Hey, what's this?" Logan asked, pointing to the wall.

"It's the same mark the girls and I saw earlier. It's an arrow with Joe's initials. Ben you recognize the way he marks his initials. He's fine. He's okay, and he's trying to find his way out of the cave," Luke explained excitedly. "Ben, we have to find him."

"Okay. I think you're right. You guys catch up with Rachael and Dori. I'm going to stay here and clear from this side. That way I can help Dad get through quicker, and we might need this tunnel to get Joe some help," Ben explained.

"Okay," said Luke as he and Logan headed back up the tunnel, keeping their eyes ready to see clues or signs. A few chalk marked arrows let them know they were on the right trail. At one marking, Logan leaned down and picked up a broken piece of chalk and handed it to Luke.

"Uh oh," said Luke. "Don't tell the girls, but I think this is a bloody fingerprint," he pointed to the dark stain on the piece of broken chalk.

✗

Joe groaned and reached his hand to his aching head, felt the soaked handkerchief, and a warm trickle running down the side of his face where the wound had reopened. He retied the bandage tighter to apply pressure, and felt for other wounds. His moist fingers revealed more cuts and scrapes, and the grit between his fingers spoke loudly with the voice of his mother, "Don't touch those open wounds with your dirty hands. You'll get germs in the wound." When he realized there were no broken bones, he felt around the ledge where he had fallen. It was a small ledge, surrounded by empty air. "I should just stay put. I'm making things worse all the time." He lay back against the wall, and caught his breath. He rested for a while, but soon decided that waiting was not easy.

He picked up a pebble from the ledge and threw it. The response didn't appear to reveal a large pit. He threw several more pebbles to make sure it was not just another ledge down below him, disguising a deep and unending pit, and satisfied that he was right, he cut a length of string from the ball he still clutched, and tied a rock to the end, and began to swing the string as he lowered it. The string stopped swinging as it came to rest on the floor of the pit.

After several more tests, Joe reeled it back up, and estimated that it was about ten feet to the floor. He could easily jump or slide to the bottom, but he would not be able to get back up. Should he try instead to go up instead of down? At the top of the precipice was a guaranteed way out of the cave. Joe felt around for a handhold to climb back out of the pit. He had often been rock climbing and was expert at finding toe holds and footholds, but this cliff wall extended out over the precipice, and Joe would be hanging from mid-air, trying to climb blindly. If he lost his grip, he would fall even further. In his weakened and bruised state, Joe thought the best way was down, and so he carefully eased his legs over the edge, and half slid, rolled, jumped to the bottom of the pit.

With relief, Joe stood to his feet, and felt his way around the pit. It was a large area, about twenty feet across, according to the tossed pebble report. So he began to follow the perimeter of the pit, looking for a tunnel opening. He went for what seemed like a mile before he realized he was going in circles. He took the length of string, and hung it from the wall, then made his way around until he came back to the string. He couldn't believe it. He had chosen to go to the depths of a pit that now imprisoned him. There was no way to escape now. He was stuck here until someone found him. Joe slumped to the floor, finally giving in to the darkness of the circumstances.

As he sat in dejection, his head cradled in his hands, the darkness of despair perched on his shoulder and whispered words of woe.

N

Rachael and Dori moved quickly through the cave, and soon arrived at the large cavern, with several tunnels merging into it.

"Wow. This room is almost as large as The Orpheum," Rachael breathed in wonder at the huge expanse and beauty of the room. She shone her flashlight around at the many cascading stalactites hanging from the ceiling. Along one wall was a curtain that extended from the ceiling to a rock platform. It looked like the curtain in a theater, with its many folds and ripples of fabric-looking stone.

"Look at the pool of water, Rachael," Dori said as she bent over a dark pool.

"Be careful, Dori, some cave pools are bottomless" Rachael shouted, as Dori leaned further over the pool.

"Look," Rachael pointed to the ceiling where thousands of bats clung to the cave surface, suspended upside down like figs on a tree.

Dori shivered, and took another step back from the edge of the pool. "Look, Rachael!" she shouted, pointing to the edge of the pool, where a footprint was embedded in the mud. "Do you think it's Joe's?"

"I'm sure it must be. Look, it's going this direction." Rachael pointed to a tunnel leading out of the cavern. They walked for a little way before the tunnel forked.

"Which way now?" Rachael asked Dori, as she swung her flashlight around in the dimly lit tunnel.

"Rachael, shine your light over here," Dori said, pointing with her own light on the ground. Rachael saw a thin string tied around a rock, with the string trailing down the tunnel.

"Looks like we go this way," Rachael said. The girls followed the string until it disappeared into a deep pit.

"Uh-oh," Rachael said with concern. She called, "Joe? Joe – are you there?" She was hesitant to shine her light into the pit, but had to. The string trailed away to a ledge just below. "Here, Dori. Follow this stairway over here. We can get almost to the bottom of the pit by going down this natural stairway." The two girls made their way carefully down the pit. Rachael handed her flashlight to Dori, and jumped the last few feet to the bottom, turning around to catch Dori as she jumped. They shone their flashlights around the pit, and Dori pointed to a string hanging from the wall. The pit seemed to be a dead-end. Rachael was surprised, "Where's Joe?"

"Shhh. Listen. Do you hear that?" Dori asked.

⚔

"The cords of the depths of the earth have coiled around me. The snares of the pit confronted me. In my distress I cried out for help." The words were spoken in a voice that was full of light and airiness that seemed to bring a bit of light into the darkness of the cavern.

As Joe realized his predicament. He had been listening to the voice of despair instead of the voice of hope. If he wanted to get out of this darkness, then he would have to reflect the light onto the situation instead of echoing the principles of darkness and blindness. He dropped to his knees.

"What a foolish, arrogant braggart I've been," he said. "I thought I had all the answers. I thought I was so smart. What an imbecile I am," he mused aloud.

"Well, I'm not going to rely on my own brains anymore. I will wait for my rescue," he said humbly. His darkened eyes were playing tricks on him. He thought he saw a dim, vapory image in front of him. He reached out for it, but it disappeared into thin air, in fact there was nothing in front of his hands – not even the cave wall.

He stood to his feet, and felt the immovable barrier of the wall of the pit.

"Hmmm," Joe said, as he felt the wall and dropped to his knees again. The wall ended at about the height of his thigh, and there was a tunnel at the level of the floor. Joe was hesitant to enter the tunnel, thinking he should just stay put. He didn't trust his own judgment. However, the glowing vapors seemed to beckon him. He heard a tinkling sound, and he knew he must follow the invitation.

Joe got on his knees and crawled for a couple yards, before the tunnel widened and enlarged enough for him to stand again. He continued walking a short distance, careful now to feel high, low, and on both sides of the tunnel to make sure he didn't miss another tunnel. Suddenly the moist, rough walls of the cave changed, and Joe felt the roughened edges of stones, mortared together.

"I've made it to the tunnel system," Joe cried with relief. "I must be close to the exit. The floor was smooth, and the walls became a guide that allowed Joe to quicken his pace. In his eagerness, Joe increased his pace until he said "Oomph," as he fell to his knees, making another bruise. His way was blocked by a stone stairway. Joe stood up, went up the stairs, and found that a large stone wall, immovable and silent blocked his way.

"Who would make a stairway to a rock wall?" Joe said aloud, and then remembered Logan's voice saying the same thing just the day before. He felt for a lever, and the door swung open. Joe took a few limping, halting steps and collapsed onto the ground in exhausted relief. He could feel the warmth of the sun on his face. His blinded eyes turned toward the sun, begging for the piercing light's assault.

"Blind. Blind. I really am blind," Joe cried. He lay back on the ground, into a soft bed of fragrant flowers, and in his blindness, Joe sensed that he was in a safe place. He calmed his recent fears, breathed in the fresh clean air, and pondered what he should do next. As he lay there in the daisies and the warmth of the sun, his recent injuries, and traumatic journey caused him to drift into a dazed slumbering dream.

It was a dream from which he never wished to awaken. His brow was caressed and bathed with water as warm as the sun. The healing water was fragrant with chamomile, and a fragrance of barberry emanated as his darkened eyes were bathed. A few drops of a bitter substance that tasted like the white fibrous skin of a grapefruit was dropped onto his tongue.

His wounds were cleansed and a healing ointment of herbs like comfrey and calendula was applied. His bruised and bloody hands were soaked in chamomile, and a healing salve massaged into his broken flesh. As he lay in relaxed repose, he dreamed that a voice of a pretty maiden was singing a song without words, but in his dream, he learned to recognize the words, as he listened to her song.

"As a drop of rain joyously joins the stream, as a single beam of sunlight joins to make the ray, even a drop rises in the sun, it joins again with others in the cloud, until it becomes rain, again to water the earth. All of the waters join together in cloud, sea and storm to refresh the land with its joy. It is joy to serve like the raindrop or the sunbeam."

"What is your name," Joe asked the beautiful ministering angel. He knew she was as beautiful as her voice and as sweet as the touch of her hand.

"Some people call me Gloria," she answered.

The lady held a cup to Joe's dry lips, and he tasted the sweetest water he'd ever known; it had a flavor of papaya. She brushed his hair from his brow, and said, "Sleep, my son. I will find your mother now." She rose and walked out of his dream. Joe thought the lady's words couldn't sound any sweeter until she said the word mother – the sweetest word a lost boy can hear.

Tears came unbidden to his eyes, and he reached up to brush them away quickly, forgetting the greasy salve on his hands. The ointment burned his eyes for a moment, and as he blinked, his eyes flashed with bursts of light, and as he lay on his back, on a bank of daisies, in a beautiful lady's garden, he saw a wondrous sight, whether in his mind as a result of the ointment, or the result of a dream precipitated by the movie set, or as a symptom of his sudden blindness and head injury, I cannot say. Joe never knew.

Suddenly he saw clouds rumbling before him -- thick black heaving swirling thunderclouds. As the clouds danced an ominously choreographed tango of trepidation, the earth trembled and quaked, and the foundations of the mountain shook; they trembled in anger. Smoke rose from a giant cauldron of calumny on the mountaintop, as two forms rose from the boiling broth of bravado into the dark skies above where Joe lay.

"I am ruler of the sky," thundered the voice of the figure who held a thunderbolt in his clenched fist.

"I am ruler of the earth and sea," roared the voice of the

trident.

"I will not share my glory with another," declared Zeus.

"I will be the supreme power," shrieked Poseidon.

As each form thundered its arrogance, it became larger and more billowing, a darker cloud of defiance.

"I can shake the foundations of the earth," boasted Poseidon as the earth rumbled and heaved, spewing lava and fiery smoke into the sky.

"I can split the skies with thunder, and hurl lightening bolts of destruction to your earth," Zeus declared.

As each entity built a monument to their magnificence, they increased in size until they filled the earth and sky. As they boasted and proclaimed their preeminence, their pedestals rose – one from the earth to the sky, the other from the sky to the earth. Each pedestal was dark with power. As the pedestals neared each other, the ferocity of the foment increased.

The earthquakes of Poseidon caused great heaving volcanoes to split open the earth and spew fiery lava and plumes of smoke into the air.

Zeus' thunderbolts ripped through the sky, licking up the waters of the ocean, producing dark heavy storm clouds that flung rain, hail and ice to put out the fiery messages of molten lava. Lightening balls hurled through the air.

"I will destroy the sky," shouted Poseidon as he raised his trident.

"I will destroy the sea and earth," shouted Zeus as he raised his fist.

Before each had opportunity to send their final crashing blow that would destroy each other's kingdom and ultimately their own in a fiery melting of the elements, their pedestals rising up from the depths and down from the heights, crashed into each other, splitting asunder and collapsing into a great and glorious demise.

Instantly the heavens parted and rolled up like a window shade does when the string is jerked and loosed, rolling up to allow the sun to stream into a gloomy darkened room. Suddenly the two fallen foes cringed in terror and slunk away in silence, like the steam from the soup trails into nothingness as you blow over the broth in your spoon.

[The mythical forms of Poseidon and Zeus were decreasing in size, strength and color. Instead of magnificent billowing storm clouds, they were a wispy white vapor, drifting aside.]

A rushing mighty wind heralded the approach of a power that soared on the wings of the wind. It made the darkness its covering and no eye could see its approach, but no ear could deny its presence. And as Joe rose to his knees to honor the approach of one who ruled the rulers, a flash of light turned everything white, and then Joe's blindness returned as he collapsed to the ground.

Chapter 17   Opere et Viritate

"What is it?" Rachael asked.

"I heard something tinkling. I heard it earlier in the library, and it led me to the library tunnel," Dori said.

"Quick. Turn off your flashlight," Rachael said. They flipped the switches on their lights, and waited for their eyes to adjust to the darkness. They stood still in the silence, and Rachael felt Dori reach for her hand. As they stood in the darkness, they heard a tinkling sound, and then in the darkness, a shimmering light began to appear. It seemed to float toward the ground, and then disappear. Rachael felt Dori pulling her hand, and followed in the dark.

Dori's hand was pulling her down, and Rachael bent over. She could see the vapors again, but they were leading her into the wall. Trusting in the vapors, Rachael followed, and instead of banging into the wall, she entered a low tunnel. She kept trusting and following the vapors, as Dori pulled her along.

Soon the vapors rose into the air, and the girls straightened up. The vapors laughed and giggled, and danced along the dark passageway, with the girls following, going up the stairs, and toward sunlight streaming into the tunnel. They tumbled into Miss Sophia's garden, bursting from the night of the cave into the brilliant light of the sunny afternoon, and their eyes were blessed with the sight they most longed for.

Dori ran to the prone body lying still as death, surrounded by a mounding bouquet of wildflowers and daisies. She stopped suddenly, afraid to approach the colorful and fragrant shroud that encompassed the still form of her brother. She turned to Rachael and whispered, "Is he – alive?"

Rachael gently felt for a pulse, and relieved Dori's concern with a nod.

"He's hurt," Dori said with compassion.

"Gloria," he mumbled. "Where is Gloria?" he asked. "Mother? Why is Gloria gone?"

"He's dreaming. I'll stay with him Dori. You go get Miss Sophia."

Dori ran off swiftly to obey.

Joe flinched at the sound of Rachael's voice, opened his eyes and said, "Who's there?"

"Joe, it's me, Rachael. Dori has gone to get help."

Joe groaned and put his hand to his brow. "It wasn't a dream. I'm really blind, Rache," he said with such sadness that it wrenched her heart.

"Don't worry, Joe. Just be still and help will be here soon," she consoled.

"I had a beautiful dream about a glorious angel who took care of me and gave me a drink and put ointment on my hands. She sang me a song, and went to get mother."

"Sounds lovely," Rachael whispered kindly.

Joe sighed wistfully, "She was. Help me get up, Rachael."

"Maybe you should lie still. You have had quite a blow to your head," Rachael remarked, observing the blood soaked headband, discarded on the ground, the gaping wound on his forehead covered with a thick salve that kept it from bleeding. He was going to need stitches.

"No. The sooner I get home, the sooner I get some help for my eyes. Just help me up, and let me lean on you, Sis."

Rachael carefully and slowly helped him to his feet, and allowed him to lean on her as she guided him through the arboretum, along the path that wound around the tower to the garden at the front of the tower.

He paused to steady himself, and said, "This is a peaceful place. I think I'd like to rest a minute. Is there some place to sit?"

"Yes, come this way. There is a nice water garden with lily pads, and colorful fish, and peaceful ripples flowing across the surface of the water. There's a handsome granite youth with a garland around his head looking over the pool," Rachael painted a picture for him as she led the way to the pool. "He kind of looks like you," she joked as she gently showed him to a concrete bench next to the pool.

"Thank you," Joe said gratefully as he eased down to the bench.

He sat for a while listening in silence to the sounds of the garden, and Rachael saw a look in his blinded eyes that she'd never noticed before. It was a look of peace, acceptance, and resignation. Joe had never been one to sit still. Mom told about how as a baby he wasn't content until he could roll over, and then not until he could crawl, and then he had to stand, and walk, and run, and climb trees, and ride a bike. There was always a next thing he had to do.

In contrast, Mom told how Ben was content to sit in her lap and be cuddled and sung to, or read to. Joe didn't like to be read to. He wanted to flip through the pictures. He had no patience for being read to, although he made up stories, and read to himself, until he taught himself to read when he was barely four. Mom told the story of how she found Joe reading to Ben one day, and thought it was so cute how he made up the story. She silently crept near for a closer look, and was astounded to find that he was reading for himself, without ever having been taught.

But, now, here was Joe, stilled by the blindness, happy to listen to the birds and the babbling of the water trickling blindly down the mountainside into the stillness of the pool, before it joined a small cascade of other drops to sweep over the edge of the pool, in a curtain that flowed into a stone basin, that flowed into another and another in a series of terraces on the hillside, before it tumbled in a miniature waterfall down the mountainside to the lake below.

Dori returned with a cool drink of water. "Miss Sophia is not here," she whispered to Rachael as she sat down beside Joe on the bench and held his hand comfortingly.

"Who is Miss Sophia?" Joe asked.

"She's the beautiful lady of the tower who helped you, and has gone to get mother," Rachael said.

"No. Her name was Gloria," Joe said with assurance. "I'm feeling a little dizzy. Would you help me lie down?" Dori shrugged her shoulders at Rachael, as though his dizziness explained his confusion.

Rachael helped him to the ground and placed his head on Dori's lap. Dori stroked his hair, and comforted him. He closed his eyes, and the sun, and Dori's gentle calming touch caused his breath to slow and deepen as he drifted to sleep. A gleam caught Dori's eye, and she noticed a golden reflection. She reached under the bench and picked up a golden-framed mirror.

"Look, Rachael," she whispered, "The mirror of truth."

"What is truth?" Joe mumbled in his sleep.

"Dori, that's not the mirror of truth. It looks like it, but the words are different. May I see it?" Rachael took the mirror and ran her fingers along the filigree scrollwork. The same scrollwork pattern adorned the entrance gate to Rhemawood, and they had seen the same design repeated in several different places here on the mountaintop. "Do you remember the words on the mirror of truth?" she asked Dori.

"Yes," Dori recited confidently, "Veritas vos liberabit."

"Yes. This says 'opere et viritate'," Rachael read slowly.

"What does it mean?" Dori asked eagerly.

"I'm not sure. Logan would know, but I think viritate is a form of veritas, which means truth," Rachael explained.

"Opere et viritate," she read again slowly.

Joe groaned and rolled his head from side to side grimacing in discomfort. He mumbled, "Actions...truth. It ain't bragging if you can do it."

"What's that mean?" Dori asked.

"He's dreaming again," Rachael explained.

"My actions do show the truth," said Joe. "I don't apologize for being good at what I do. I work hard to be the best. I never say anything about my accomplishments that isn't true," Joe argued in his sleep. Suddenly Joe opened his eyes, sat up, and took the mirror from Dori's hand. He gazed into it fiercely with his sightless eyes.

Rachael watched the features of his face react to what he saw reflected in the mirror.

"What can he see with blinded eyes?" Rachael wondered.

"The mirror shows you what you really are. Everyone sees something different when they look into the reflection," Dori wisely answered.

Rachael hushed Dori as Joe began to speak like someone telling a story, the mirror cradled in his hands like a treasure.

Chapter 18   Parable of the Gardener

A gardener planted two seeds in separate corners of his garden. Both seeds were dusty, brown, and wrinkled, and the gardener planted them, watered them, and as they grew he pruned and tended them. Soon, the one tree consumed the gardener's time. He trained the branches to grow in a beautiful way, and tenderly watched over it during each season. He placed beehives at the base of the tree to pollinate the blossoms. He carried bucketfuls of mulch to surround the base of the tree.

"He cut the branches away to keep the strongest, most beautiful ones, and as it began to bear vibrant fruit, he inspected it, and plucked it, collecting many heaping baskets of juicy fruit year after year. Some seasons he would light torches around the base of the tree to protect the tender blossoms from the icy tentacles of the frosty air. Sometimes he filled pots with smoking pesticides to chase away a plague of insects. If the branches were heavy with fruit, he propped them up to keep from cracking the branches, or he picked off the smaller, defective fruits to allow the best and brightest to thrive.

"Meanwhile the other tree was forgotten and ignored. It grew with a crooked and thick trunk. Its branches were not pruned, and its trunk wrapped around, twisted and thickened until it was a massive tree with roots so thick and strong there wasn't room in the earth to contain them. They burst from the ground and nestled themselves at the base of the tree. The long boughs of the tree hung low as though to hide in shame the thick, ugly tangle of branches beneath the weeping willows.

"This tree received no special attention. In fact, one year, during a wicked ice storm, while the gardener worked night and day to protect the branches and blooms of the fruit tree, this one, accustomed to bending and swaying in the storms of life, had bowed beneath a heavy load of ice for days with no relief, and as the ice began to melt, and the birds began to reappear, this tree remained bowed in submission to the result of the weight of the burden – now removed but forever remembered.

"The tree remained deformed, and yet it burst forth in the appropriate season with new branches, new leaves, and renewed determination to be all the gardener meant for it. Only those privileged to enter the inner sanctum would see the sacrifice of the scarred and broken back of the tree.

"If you walk through this garden on a sunny day, at a particular time when the sun is beginning to paint the sky goodbye, you will see the dirt-caked work boots of the gardener peeking from beneath a canopy of willow curtain of the tree that had been abandoned to nature, and if you pull back the curtain, quietly, so you don't disturb, you will see the gardener stretched out with his back cradled against the trunk and roots, his hat pulled over his face, a slight smile tilting the corners of his lips, while the birds sing a symphony, with the bees humming a harmony. The wind whispers through the boughs of the branches, and there lies an apple core in the gardener's hand, a remnant of the vibrant red at each end of the core, and the gardener is pleased with his trees – one a mark of pride and distinguishing beauty, the other a source of solace and serenity, both loved and cherished by the gardener.

Which seed was more valuable to the gardener? Which tree brought him greatest pleasure? To whom belongs the glory of the garden? How does the gardener assign value and worth to his trees? Is it in beauty or in the pleasure they bring him?"

As Rachael listened in rapt attention to the beautiful parable, Luke and Logan silently joined the group at the water's edge. As Joe finished his story, he cradled his head on his arms as he sat on the stones beside the pool, resting his arms on the concrete bench, the mirror sliding from his fingers.

The four children moved to a distance for a conference.

"Is he okay?" Logan asked with concern.

"I don't know. It's like he's in a dream-like state," Rachael replied.

"Delirious?" Luke asked.

"Not really. Kind of lost in his own world. He seems to be struggling within himself," Rachael explained.

"What do you mean?" Luke asked.

"Well, it's almost like he's arguing with himself," Rachael said.

"About what?" Logan asked.

"About pride and humility, and arrogance and glory," Rachael replied, looking with concern to Joe's bowed head. "Truth and blindness. He can't see. His eyes were injured in the explosion, and yet he seems to be seeing things in a different world."

"What do you mean?" Logan asked.

"His eyes are open to truths we cannot see with our own eyes in this world," Rachael said.

"A man's pride brings him low," Logan quoted.

"What do you mean?" Rachael asked.

"It's an old proverb, kind of like, 'Pride goeth before a fall'," said Luke.

"Or be careful you don't get knocked off your high horse," Logan joked.

"There is something about seeing someone step high on a

pedestal that invites a toppling," Luke said.

"Yeah, like the statue in the abbey courtyard," Dori giggled.

Luke suddenly rose to his feet and walked to the stone figure that stood watch over the pool, next to the concrete bench where Joe rested. He traced the banner, which wound from its shoulder, draped across its chest, and ended where the bust was mounted on a pedestal with ivy entwined from the ground, around the base and climbing to encircle his head with a laurel crown.

Luke carefully pulled back the ivy drape to reveal the banner. He traced the letters on the banner.

Dori, followed him, and read the letters. "J, O," she said.

Logan crept up for a closer look. "Hey, this bust is a broken piece from another statue," he said excitedly to Luke who nodded knowingly. "See the jagged edge at the bottom?" he said as he rocked the stone head back and forth.

"Careful, or it will topple from its pedestal," said Rachael.

"Hey," said Logan just beginning to guess what Luke already knew. 'This is the other half of that statue we saw in the abbey courtyard. See this would be the head, and fit together, and so the word on the banner would be --," he thought.

"Joseph," Dori said, looking toward her brother as he rose to his knees and faced the heavens.

"The heavens have opened to reveal the glory of another realm again," Rachael said.

"Well, we've been here before," Logan said. "Where there was a different reality going on than we could see with our eyes. You remember how the garden looked before it was restored to its original glory?"

"Well, technically we've been here in this garden in a different realm, but not this particular realm," Luke said. "We don't know where Joe really is."

"How do we get Joe back to seeing the reality of our eyes?" Rachael asked.

"Do we want to?" Dori asked, from her post next to Joe.

"Of course. We can't let him stay blind," Logan said.

"He might not see the pool and the flowers we see, but he sees a whole other world that is beautiful and wise," Dori said seriously.

"Maybe we should leave him there for awhile until he figures out what he needs to learn," Logan said.

"That other world is as real as ours, but Joe was born for this world, and as long as he's here, he needs eyes to see and ears to hear what is in this world," Luke said. "We'll just have to help him figure it out."

Dori picked up the mirror that slipped through Joe's fingers as he dozed again. She looked into the mirror and gasped, "Look everyone." She held up the mirror and they looked within, but the reflection they saw mirrored back to them wasn't the garden with the pool where they currently sat, it was the garden Joe had described in his story. Joe had only described the two trees. He hadn't described the full beauty of the garden. Rare varieties of flowers and birds and butterflies flitting from color to color, and statues on pedestals, and flowing fountains, and something else, too.

Clear vapor beings danced among the flowers. They collected the fragrance of the flowers, and when the vapors were full of fragrance, like a hot air balloon rises when the air within is sufficiently heated, they rose into the air, a transparent snowflake-shaped bubble, filled with visible fragrance.

The vapors rose on the beams of sunlight, like a cloud, like a water molecule rises on evaporating rays of sunlight to the clouds, these vapors rose and became a translucent cloud of color, fragrance and music in the sky. As they joined together in unison, their colors, fragrances and sounds blended into a mighty orchestra of colorful fragrance that permeated the air, reverberating clarity and purity, a swirling sunset alive with sound.

The greatest joy of these beings, was to join together to create a new sunrise, a new song, or a new tapestry in the heavens. Even a single drop of water cannot ascend to the heavens; it must decrease in order to be elevated. It must condense in order to evaporate and ascend to the heights. It must disappear into nothing we can see, in order to join with millions of other water molecules to create a cloud. And they keep going, keep growing, keep inviting, keep expanding until in one beautiful moment, the cloud is fully saturated and then many molecules become a droplet once more and descend in a dizzying exhilaratingly lonely rush with others, separate from the cloud, but together in the rain, to their home on earth once again.

As the children watched this phenomenon in the mirror, the beautiful vapor clouds began to grow darker in color, and suddenly a bolt crashed through the vapors to the ground – a rainbow lightening bolt, accompanied by a thunderous shout of acclamation that seemed to shout, "Gloria!"

Dori, startled by the thunder, jumped and dropped the mirror, which shattered at her feet. She gasped and burst into tears. "I've broken the only link with Joe's world. Now Joe will never see again in this world of ours," she cried.

"Don't cry, Dori. Don't worry. Miss Sophia always has another mirror for another time," Rachael comforted the girl's sobs.

"Okay," said Luke, wanting to get back to the business of helping Joe. "We know that Joe is trapped in a world where he can see other things. In our world he is blind."

"How do we bring him back to our world? To see things clearly again?" Logan asked.

"And what does Joe need to learn before truth will be revealed?" Rachael asked.

"I think it has something to do with all of this," said Logan, reviewing his notebook where he had been taking notes. "Pride, arrogance, glory, falling from a pedestal."

"I have been blinded by my arrogance, unable to see a true reflection of the effects of pride on my actions," Joe responded to Logan, although he seemed to be speaking to himself. Even though he was interacting with them, it was as if a veil separated their two worlds. They were living the same moment, sharing the same physical spaces, but two different worlds were revealed to Joe and to his siblings.

"What do you mean, Joe?" Logan asked his brother. Joe did not respond. Logan shook his shoulder. "Joe, can you hear me?" Joe didn't answer.

Luke, who had been thinking seriously, came up with an idea, and approached Joe, and although speaking at him, wasn't speaking to him. He said, "Pride brings a man low, but the humble man is raised up."

Joe did not seem to hear Luke, or realize that he was right next to him, yet he said, "In the glory of my pride, I have not been elevated, but I am at the lowest point of my life. Only when I decrease, am I able to really rise to new heights of success."

"Pride causes quarrels, but wisdom is found in those who take advice," Luke said, and then paused.

Joe was lost in silent reflection, and then began to speak,

"My arrogance has caused me to have conflict with those I love most. I should know better. Dad always has good advice. He is very wise, and I should learn to listen to him," he said.

"Pride blinds us to the truth," Luke said.

Joe sat silently, staring blindly around, groping with his hands, "I am blinded in my eyes, but more importantly, my heart has been blinded to the truth. Because of my arrogance, I let Mr. Ubsen have the Flying Flambé, I misinterpreted Dad, and I failed to do my job."

"Arrogance causes us to receive an improper echo of the real world," Rachael added, realizing that Joe, although not on their same wavelength, was still occupying the same physical area, and was receiving messages through the veil that separated them.

Logan realized what Rachael was doing and added excitedly, "Like a bat."

"Like a bat uses echolocation to 'see' his surroundings, I need to be aware of my world, and to listen to the feedback I receive from other people. When my pride gets in the way, then I become blind to the signals that would help me to interact properly in my world," Joe said.

"Humble thyself, and be lifted up," Logan quoted.

"If I will allow myself to stop seeking acclamation, and bend myself low, then I am free to receive success, and be raised up," Joe said.

"The penitent man will pass," Dori quoted.

"When I bow down to the circumstances of my life, and allow the purposes of a greater good to shape my life, then I can be free to seek purity and a plan that benefits everyone," Joe said.

"People don't care how much you know, until they know how much you care," Dori said, repeating her favorite quote.

"I have been arrogantly proclaiming my superiority instead of paying attention to the people around me," Joe said.

"You have to be willing to be the willow tree and not demand to be the fruit tree," Dori said with wisdom beyond her years.

Suddenly Joe stood to his feet, and his sightless eyes searched the sky in wonder.

"Shhh. He sees something," Luke said, motioning to the others to stay back and remain quiet.

Chapter 19   How Many Apples Are in a Seed?

Like shadows on a curtain, or a shout through a waterfall, there was a distortion between their realms, but a semblance of the reality was reflected to Joe. The wisdom of his brothers and sisters had to travel through a thick veil, but the message was coming through. And now all the voices that he'd heard that day came back to teach him one last lesson.

The forms of Poseidon and Zeus appeared, but suddenly a voice thundered from the darkness, a voice that wrapped itself in the darkness that it ruled, and the darkness was dissolved in the light of its voice, "Who is this who seeks to darken wisdom with thundering of pride?" it questioned the mythical pretenders.

"Can a created figment of imagination dare to proclaim the wisdom of the ages?"

"Is a shadow real? Can it exist without the light?"

How many stars are in the sky? Can you call them all by

name?

Can you stop the orbit of the earth around the sun or visit another galaxy?

What language do the stars speak? Can you understand their voice?

Does the tornado choose the path it sews along in the seam of the garment of destruction?

Can the rumble of your voice cause the earthquake or the tsunami?

Can you calm the storm with your voice?

Can you call the winds to change the temperature?

"Does the rain fall on the just and the unjust?

While the voice spoke, Poseidon and Zeus trembled and began to dissolve in mortification.

The voice spoke to Joe. "You, who are a mass of multiplied millions of cells living in a world of swirling neutrons and protons, can you create even one tiny atom?

"Can one who cannot create an atom assume to proclaim in arrogance how it was created?"

Can you lead the monarch to the same garden where its grandfather was born?

Do you know the route to send the carrier pigeon home?

Do you know why a salmon can go between salt water and fresh?

Can you hear the heart of the humpback whale?

Can you tell me where the brontosaurus came from and to where it has gone, and how it lived in between?

Can you tell me if reptiles can fly in the air or swim in the ocean?

Who calls for the cicada, buried in the ground for thirteen years, to come forth?

Tell me if you know.

"Who made you? Did you create yourself? Can you speak light from the dark? Can you make something visible from things that are not seen? Can you breathe life into dust?"

Suddenly the gardener appeared, and held an apple seed out to Joe. "Can you turn a seed into an apple?" He closed Joe's fingers around the seed, and the gardener asked, "How many apples are in a seed?" The gardener turned and walked away, and in his footsteps a message appeared, the words took flight, and the message spoke aloud, "Why are atoms attracted to each other? What keeps electrons spinning in their orbits? Why does water travel to the sky and back again just to please you? Why does blood carry oxygen? Why do you die without air? Where do you go when your breath ceases? Where does your heart beat go when you die? Tell me if you know. Does your knowledge alter the laws of nature? Can you change gravity?"

"Stop!" Joe cried, putting his hands to his ears.

"Don't stop your ears from hearing, or your eyes from seeing. Do stop your mouth from speaking. Listen and watch.

It is true that you are blind. There is a whole world you do not see. Look!" Suddenly Joe's eyes were opened to the unseen world that surrounded him. He saw atoms of carbon, oxygen and hydrogen swirling around him in an ocean of air that he'd never observed. In that ocean was a whole ecosystem, which he'd learned of in science class, but had never seen. It had been there all the time, but he had not had eyes to see that the elements were involved in an intricately choreographed dance of delight as two hydrogen atoms joined hands with an oxygen atom and twirled together, their colors melding into another hue as the three became one. They were made up of textures, hues, sounds and smells of which he'd never known, and he knew his eyes would never tire of seeing them.

He looked into the garden at a group of butterflies fluttering around a bed of flowers. But no, those weren't flowers they were fluttering around. Their delicate wings were wistful brushes. The flapping of their wings was producing a colorful haze that painted a picture in the air. With their movements, they created a magnificent Monet of watercolor delights.

"You have ears, but there is a whole world that you do not hear. Listen!" Suddenly Joe's ears were attune to the sound waves of color and water and sunlight. As the sunlight washed over him in golden waves of warmth and light, he heard its ebb and flow. The colors of the garden lifted their instruments of praise, and performed a symphony of color. The water molecules in the air tickled his cheek, and suddenly, like the secret sound of the ocean in a cockleshell, he heard the tidal wave of the air whispered in his ear.

The sounds of the buzzing bees sent up a waving web-like strand that danced together with the silky sound wave spun by the singing of the birds. The trickling water tossed up a tendril of glistening gossamer that was woven with the threads of the other sounds of creation into a tapestry of beautiful textures, spinning a story that was too glorious to evolve.

"You are too finite to see and hear and touch all that has been created for your pleasure. Touch the world in which you live. Feel!" Suddenly the molecules of water in the air bathed him in vibrations of living sound, color and fragrance. The colors of the garden rushed to caress him with a touch that stimulated each skin cell and hair follicle, and he could breath in the colors of the garden. The colors danced in his brain, and the fragrance sang on his synapses.

"There is a whole world to taste that you have not consumed. Taste and see that it is good!"

Joe opened his mouth and tasted the color of a violet, the buzzing of a bee, the fluttering of a butterfly, a ray of sunlight, and a whispering wind. His taste buds throbbed with the sensations of the taste of delicacies he had never known could be sampled.

As Joe took in the wonder of this new old world around him,

a vapor came near, as though to kiss his cheek, and whispered a question in a still small voice, "What does fragrance look like?" As the vapor asked the question, it gained momentum to rise into the ocean of the air, until it gathered together into a great rainbow cloud in the heavens. This was not a catatonic cumulus cloud, but a colorful cloud alive with vibrancy, undulating with liquid energy.

Thousands of other vapors drew near to question him.

"What does Cyrillian blue smell like? What does a Beethoven symphony taste like? What sound would a beautiful sunset make? What fragrance would you ascribe to the morning hues of a brilliant sunrise? How would you dance if unencumbered by weight and gravity? Would you leap and glide and float and somersault and tumble in the air before you learned to fly?"

As each vapor asked its question, a wondrous event occurred. The vapor, as alive and beautiful as it was, with iridescent prism-like colors reflecting all the spectrum of the rainbow, went through a wondrous metamorphosis. A rainbow lightening bolt appeared in the multifaceted sphere-like shape. As it flickered and flashed, crackled and crashed, the vapor was illuminated with energy that created and revealed a golden liquid filling the vapor. The liquid came alive with the energy of the rainbow storm, and as each bolt illuminated the sphere, a color was struck like a chime, and it permeated the vapor with swirling designs in the golden liquid. As the blasts continued, the colors mixed and merged creating streaks of hues and tints that were embossed with gold.

Then in rapturous joy, the vapor ascended with a shout to meet the cloud in the air, to join with it in complete joy in the unity of their purpose – to create a living work of art – to paint a portrait in the heavens, a new creature of beauty – a momentary reflection of an infinitely intense moment of majesty.

Joe watched this symphony for one, and said, "I had glimpses of glory in my imagination, but now I see them with my eyes – a sight too glorious for speech, and so I place my hand over my mouth to stop my tongue from speaking things too wonderful for words."

Suddenly a rainbow blast of brilliance came from the cloud and struck the ground near Joe. The earth trembled and shook, and Joe felt the wave of the energy, but heard no sound of thunder. This pure energy needed no echo of acclamation – it spoke for itself in wonder, power and magnificence.

Another bolt hit the ground at Joe's feet, and he fell to his knees. A third bolt was dispatched, but this bolt, like brontide didn't hit the ground, but came straight through the air, splitting through the atmosphere in a horizontal stream of energy. It circled Joe, and rose into the air before turning sharply, aiming straight for Joe. He did not flinch in fear, but raised his face in faith, knowing that this moment was meant for him.

Suddenly a vapor appeared between him and the bolt. The vapor whispered a question of the bolt, "Is anything too difficult for you?" and the question expanded to fill the vapor with glowing liquid. With a sudden force that was more than the vapor could absorb, the bolt struck the vapor. The bolt pierced the vapor, and the vapor was rent in two, and the liquid energy within flowed with harmonious tones as it wept upon Joe's head like a healing, cleansing, baptism of fire. The energy flowed like anointing oil upon Joe's head, down his brow, cascading into his eyes, and onto his shoulders. The liquid energy was warm and tingling, and Joe felt all the synapses of his body crackle and jump with the energy.

Joe realized that the heavenly vision with the lightening bolt of energy that had appeared to his blinded eyes was gone, and instead his eyes were now regaining their natural sight. His open eyes saw light and color through the stream of flowing energy, and as the liquid energy flowed away from his eyes, the natural world began to take shape. He saw great giants swaying as the trees began to assume their natural form and clap their hands. A blur of rainbow colors, reminiscent of Monet's Impression Sunrise or his Garden Path, or his Bridge Over a Pond of Water Lilies, came into focus as the flowers lifted their petals to rejoice, and the birds stood at attention on the tree branches, shouting their song of acclamation, and then the pond of water lilies became real as he focused on the pool in the garden where he stood.

Joe staggered to his feet as he shouted, "I once was lost, but now am found, was blind, but now I see."

Luke and Logan ran to him, and Dori jumped into his arms as Rachael hugged him, laughing and crying at the same moment. Mom and Dad and Ben hurried down the garden path, led by Miss Sophia to their lost boy, and soon the whole family was rejoicing to have the lamb returned to the fold.

Miss Sophia spread a table before them in the garden, and they celebrated teatime together.

"Oh thank you, Miss Sophia," Dori said. I was hoping that Ben and Joe could meet you. Miss Sophia smiled and said, "But I have met Joseph and Benjamin already; I have known them for many years." Both boys raised their eyes in surprise.

Rachael said, "Miss Sophia, thank you for serving us tea in your garden."

"It is joy to serve," she said with a gracious bow. Joe looked up suddenly at the beautiful lady. He recognized her voice as the one from his dream. She handed him a china plate heaped full of slices of fruit bread. "I thought your name was Gloria?" he said.

"I am known by names," she said with a smile.

As Joe took a slice of bread, he noticed the Latin phrase entwined in ivy on the plate, "Opere et Viritate," he read.

His dad said, "In action –"

His mother finished "--and truth."

Miss Sophia said, "Your actions will reflect the truth of your character, children."

"I'm sorry that Jacobson got your Flying Flambé', son. I had out Human Resources Department crosscheck his credentials, and he is a relative of Tom Jacobson and works for Colossal Creations. I don't know what his plans are, but they're certainly not ethical, and I'm not sure what we can do. He can analyze the formula, and recreate the design under a new name, and we really can't stop him. We have no evidence to report."

"That's okay, Dad. It was just one design. The new timing device I've developed wasn't even installed in that unit. Besides, there are a lot more ideas where that came from," he said confidently.

Every eye pivoted to him in concern at his words of confidence, knowing where his pride had led him this day.

He reassured them, "None of my ideas were uniquely mine, and I can't take credit for anything spectacular. Man cannot really create anything new. We just take the elements and combine them in new and interesting ways. We duplicate things we see in the awesome creation, and take the building blocks that were intricately and uniquely designed on our beautiful planet to either build new monuments to our arrogance, or to glorify our creator. Dad, I have so many new ideas for fireworks after today. You have no idea what research I've been doing this afternoon into pyrotechnics and explosives. The sky really is the limit," he said excitedly as Dori giggled at his pun.

"Dad, do you know how to make liquid gold, or a rainbow cloud, or a prism lightening bolt?" his words tumbled over each other in his eagerness.

"I don't know," Dad said, grinning at all his questions. "Do you know how many apples are in a seed?" he asked in return.

Joe's jaw dropped, as he opened his hand that had remained clenched at his side during teatime. He held it out for everyone to see the seed lying in his hand. "I don't know, but does anyone want to help me find out?" He said with a gleaming challenge in his eye.

Soli Deo Gloria

Glossary

Acclamation: a loud shout or other demonstration of welcome, goodwill, or approval.

Accompaniment: The musical background provided for a main part.

Anvil: a heavy iron block with a smooth face, frequently of steel, on which metals, usually heated until soft, are hammered into desired shapes.

Anomaly: a deviation from the common rule, type, arrangement, or form.

Arboretum: a plot of land on which many different trees or shrubs are grown for study or display.

Arsenal: A place for storing, or a collection of ammunition, arms or military equipment.

Ascended: to move, climb, or go upward; mount; rise.

Asunder: into separate parts; in or into pieces.

Bar-B-Que: meat roasted over an open hearth; commonly basted with sauce; also spelled barbecue, BBQ, barbeque

Baton: A wand used by a conductor.

Bellows: a device for producing a strong current of air, consisting of a chamber that can be expanded to draw in air through a valve and contracted to expel it through a tube, used to add oxygen to a fire in order to make it burn hotter.

Beethoven: Ludwig van Beethoven, 1770–1827, German composer, who composed even after he became deaf.

Bentonite: an absorbent clay, which expands to several times its mass when wet, making it useful as a sealant.

Blue dye: bluing, a substance, as indigo, used to whiten clothes or give them a bluish tinge.

Brass: The family of wind instruments made of brass or other metal in which the player's lips serve as the reed, i.e. lip-vibrated aerophones, namely the trumpet, trombone, French horn, and tuba.

Bravado: a pretentious, swaggering display of courage.

Bromelain: an ingredient from grapefruit, taken internally to aid in getting rid of black eyes.

Brontes: A figure from Greek mythology; a son of Uranus and Gaia, brother to Arges and Steropes, who forged the thunderbolt for Zeus, the trident for Poseidon, and the helmet for Hades.

Bust: a sculptured, painted, drawn, or engraved representation of the upper part of the human figure, esp. a portrait sculpture showing only the head and shoulders of the subject.

Calcium Carbonate: a white, crystalline, water-insoluble, tasteless powder, $CaCO_3$, occurring in nature in various forms, as calcite, chalk, and limestone:

Calliope: literally means beautifully voiced; the ninth and chief muse, presiding over eloquence and epic poetry, from Greek mythology.

Calumny: a false and malicious statement designed to injure the reputation of someone or something.

Catatonic: Muscular rigidity, frozen, zombie-like.

Cauldron: A large kettle or boiler.

Caving Protocol: Caves can be dangerous places: hypothermia, falling, flooding, and physical exhaustion are the main risks. To be safe: check for risk of flooding, explore caves in teams, notify outside persons of location, and estimated time of return, use hands-free lighting of at least 2-3 sources, wear appropriate clothing, and mark the trail, and remember to protect the cave environment.

Centrifugal: moving or directed outward from the center.

Chemistry: The science that deals with the composition and properties of substances and various elementary forms of matter The knowledge of chemistry is beneficial in many fields, and everyone should learn as much as possible so you can be knowledgeable about your world and how it relates to your life and your body..

Choreographed: to manage and arrange the intricate steps or routine.

Cicada: An insect in which the nymph stage remains buried underground in a life cycle that can be thirteen or seventeen years in the United States. This life cycle, (which is a prime number) allows the cicada to avoid the predatory insects with a shorter life cycle of less than two years.

Clapperboard: Boards held in front of a movie camera and banged together to show scene and take number, used in 'old days' to synchronize sound and motion picture.

Comfrey: Herb used to promote healing of cuts, bruises and wounds.

Crescendo: An Italian musical term that indicates to the musician to increase the loudness.

Conductor: Director of a performing group to coordinate all parts in aspect to time and presentation.

Cumulus: Resembling a pile or mound; heaped up.

Cupola: A dome-like structure; a light structure on a dome or roof, serving as a belfry, lantern, or belvedere.

Dean, Dizzy: 1911–74, U.S. baseball pitcher, quoted as saying, "It ain't bragging if you can do it."

Debut: A French word that refers to the first appearance before the public of an actor.

Demise: Death, termination of existence or operation

Disembodied: to get rid of the body.

Doppler: named after Austrian physicist Christian **Doppler** who proposed it in 1842, is the change in frequency of a wave for an observer moving relative to the source.

Drum Cadence: a rhythmic work played exclusively by the percussion section of a marching band to provide a beat to marchers.

Dubious: Doubtful, of uncertain outcome.

Dynamo Flashlight: a flashlight that does not require standard batteries, but gets its energy from a handle that turns gears and generates a direct current of electricity for the bulb.

Echolocation: the sonar-like system used by dolphins, bats, and other animals to detect and locate objects by emitting usually high-pitched sounds that reflect off the object and return to the animal's ears or other sensory receptors.

Embossed: To decorate with raised ornament, outline.

Ensemble: A group of musicians performing together.

Euridice: the wife of Orpheus, who was bitten by a poisonous snake on their wedding day. He traveled to Hades to bring her back, on the condition that she could return as long as he didn't look at her until they got back to sunlight. He failed, and she returned to Hades forever.

Fidelity: Strict observance of promises, loyalty, faithfulness.

Filigree: delicate ornamental work of fine silver, gold, or other metal wires, esp. lacy jewelers' work of scrolls and arabesques.

Flambe: Served flaming and ignited.

Foment: To instigate or foster discord or rebellion.

Forge: a special fireplace, hearth, or furnace in which metal is heated before shaping; the workshop of a blacksmith; smithy.

Formidable: Of great force, powerful, causing fear or dread.

Fraught: Filled with or accompanied by.

Garland: a wreath or festoon of flowers, leaves, or other material, worn for ornament or as an honor or hung on something as a decoration.

Gossamer: a fine, filmy cobweb seen on grass or bushes or floating in the air in calm weather, any thin light fabric.

Granite: a coarse-grained igneous rock composed chiefly of orthoclase and albite feldspars and of quartz, usually with lesser amounts of one or more other minerals, as mica, hornblende, or augite.

Hades: In classical Greek mythology, the underworld, or the ruler of the underworld.

Hesiod: 8th century BC Greek poet

Homer: 9th-century BC, Greek epic poet: reputed author of the Iliad and Odyssey.

Humpback Whale Songs: The males produce a complex whale song that lasts for up to ten minutes and can be repeated for hours at a time. The purpose of the song is not clear, but seems to be a way of communicating with other whales. Some scientists hypothesize that the song may serve as an echolocation function, and may also keep migrating populations connected. They have no vocal cords, so the sound is produced by forcing air through their massive nasal cavities.

Illuminated: To light up.

Impression Sunrise: Claude Monet's painting gave rise to the Impressionist Movement

Iridescent: a play of lustrous changing colors.

Laurel: A bay tree, a victor's wreath, an honor or achievement.

Law of Gravity: Described by Isaac Newton; what goes up must come down.

Lightening Ball: The term refers to reports of luminous, usually spherical objects which vary from pea-sized to several meters in diameter

Limestone: a sedimentary rock consisting predominantly of calcium carbonate.

Lyre: a musical instrument of ancient Greece consisting of a soundbox made typically from a turtle shell, with two curved arms connected by a yoke from which strings are stretched to the body, used esp. to accompany singing and recitation.

Maxwell, John C.: Attributed with the quote "People don't care how much you know, until they know how much you care".

MRE: Abbreviation for Meals Ready to Eat, prepackaged food used by the armed forces in combat.

Metamorphosis: a profound change in form from one stage to the next in the life history of an organism, as from the caterpillar to the pupa and from the pupa to the adult butterfly.

Monet, Claude: 1840–1926, French painter.

Muse: a goddess presiding over an art; any of a number of sister goddesses, originally given as Aoede (song), Melete (meditation), and Mneme (memory), but latterly and more commonly as the nine daughters of Zeus and Mnemosyne who presided over various arts: Calliope (epic poetry), Clio (history), Erato (lyric poetry), Euterpe (music), Melpomene (tragedy), Polyhymnia (religious music), Terpsichore (dance), Thalia (comedy), and Urania (astronomy)

Negate: To deny or nullify.

Negative Integer: Numbers less than zero.

Newton, Sir Isaac: 1642–1727, English philosopher and mathematician: formulator of the law of gravitation.

Night Blindness: At night, the flash produced by ignition of gunpowder can cause temporary night-blindness by photo-bleaching visual purple (the pigment of the retina that is responsible for the formation of photoreceptor cells and initial perception of light; exposed to light, the pigment immediately photo-bleaches and it takes about thirty minutes to regenerate fully in humans).

Nymph: beautiful maidens inhabiting the sea, rivers, woods, trees, mountains, and meadows.

Ominous: Threatening evil or harm.

Opere et viritate: Latin phrase; In action and truth.

Opulent: Richly supplied, abundant or plentiful.

Orpheum: A large theater.

Orpheus: Greek Legend. a poet and musician, a son of Calliope, who followed his dead wife, Eurydice, to the underworld. By charming Hades, he obtained permission to lead her away, provided he did not look back at her until they returned to earth. But at the last moment he looked, and she was lost to him forever.

Papaya: the large, yellow, melonlike fruit of a tropical American shrub or small tree, eaten raw or cooked; can be used medicinally as an aid in soothing black eyes and abrasions.

Pedestal: an architectural support for a column, statue, vase, or the like.

Peerotechnics: a mispronunciation of pyrotechnics (the art of making fireworks or using them in a dramatic display).

Perimeter: Border or outer boundary.

Periodic Table: a table illustrating the periodic system, in which the chemical elements, formerly arranged in the order of their atomic weights and now according to their atomic numbers are shown in related groups.

Permeated: to be diffused through; pervade; saturate.

Piece de resistance: The most noteworthy or prized aspect of an event. Pronounced in English as pee-es duh ri-zee-stahns.

Phosphorus: A chemical element used on match heads to produce a flame.

Pinatas: a gaily decorated crock or papier-mâché figure filled with toys, candy, etc., and suspended from above, esp. during birthday festivities, so that children, who are blindfolded, may break it or knock it down with sticks and release the contents.

Poseidon: the ancient Greek ruler of the sea, with the power to cause earthquakes, identified by the Romans with Neptune.

Potassium Nitrate: a chemical compound with the notation KNO3, commonly called saltpeter, and used as an ingredient in fireworks, rocket propellants, and as a fertilizer.

Preceding: previous, occurring earlier. Precede is not to be confused with proceed, which means to carry on, or to go forth.

Prism: a transparent solid body, often having triangular bases, used for dispersing light into a spectrum or for reflecting rays of light.

Pyrotechnics: The art of making fireworks or explosives, or using them in creative display.

Pyrotechnic safety: Using fireworks and explosives is a dangerous activity; only use fireworks and explosives under the direct supervision of your parents, Making fireworks and explosives is a complex scientific art and should only be attempted under proper supervision, training and/or proper certification..

Rapturous: full of, feeling, or manifesting ecstatic joy or delight.

Reverberated: To reecho or resound, to be reflected many times as a sound wave.

Rodin's 'The Thinker': 1840–1917, Francois Rodin, Auguste Rene: French sculptor; 'The Thinker' is a bronze statue of a man with his chin on his hand, presumably in pensive thought.

Roman Doric: Doric columns stood directly on the flat pavement of a temple without a base; their vertical shafts were fluted with 20 parallel concave grooves; and they were topped by a smooth capital.

Schuller, Robert is attributed with the quote, "Anyone can count the seeds in an apple, but only God can count the apples in a seed."

Score: A notation showing all the parts of an ensemble, arranged one underneath another on different staves.

Sentry: a soldier stationed at a place to stand guard and prevent the passage of unauthorized persons, or watch for fires.

Sextant: an astronomical instrument used to determine latitude and longitude at sea by measuring angular distances, esp. the altitudes of sun, moon, and stars.

Sforzando: An Italian musical term that instructs the musician to give a sudden strong accent on a single note or chord.

Shakespeare, William: 1564-1616, a poet and playwright.

Shroud: a cloth or sheet in which a corpse is wrapped for burial.

Siblings: brothers or sisters.

Sledge: A heavy hammer used to pound with crushing blows.

Sodium Nitrate: the chemical compound with the formula $NaNO_3$, also known as nitratine or soda niter is used as an ingredient in fireworks, food preservatives, glass and pottery.

Sodium Nitrite: a chemical compound with the chemical notation $NaNO_2$, that is commonly used as a color fixative and preservative in meat and fish. It is slowly oxidized in air to sodium nitrate, $NaNO_3$.

Sonar: a method for detecting and locating objects submerged in water by echolocation.

Spectrum: an array of entities, as light waves or particles, ordered in accordance with the magnitudes of a common physical property, as wavelength or mass: often the band of colors produced when sunlight is passed through a prism, comprising red, orange, yellow, green, blue, indigo, and violet.

Spelunking: Exploring caves. Caves can be dangerous places: hypothermia, falling, flooding, and physical exhaustion are the main risks. To be safe: check for risk of flooding, explore caves in teams, notify outside persons of location, and estimated time of return, use hands-free lighting of at least 2-3 sources, wear appropriate clothing, mark the trail, and remember to protect the cave environment.

Sphere: any rounded body like a ball.

Stalactite: a deposit, usually of calcium carbonate, shaped like an icicle, hanging from the roof of a cave or the like, and formed by the dripping of percolating calcareous water.

Symphony: A composition for an orchestra.

Synapses: a region where nerve impulses are transmitted and received, in response to an impulse.

Syncopation: A momentary contradiction of the prevailing meter.

TMI: texting abbreviation for "too much information".

Tango: a ballroom dance of Latin-American origin, danced by couples, and having many varied steps, figures, and poses.

Tempo: the speed of a composition.

Three-headed Beast of Hades: The dog who guarded the entrance to Hades.

Timpani: kettle drums; a basin-shaped shell of copper or brass over which is stretched a head of calfskin, whose tension can be adjusted by screws thereby changing the pitch.

Trajectory: the curve of a rocket in flight.

Translucent: permitting light to pass through but diffusing it so that persons, objects, etc., on the opposite side are not clearly visible.

Traversed: a series of intersecting lines and angles.

Trepidation: tremulous fear, alarm, or agitation; perturbation.

Trident: the three-pronged spear forming a characteristic attribute of the sea ruler Poseidon, or Neptune.

Undulating: to have a wavy form or surface; bend with successive curves in alternate directions.

Unison: One sound.

Unknown Number: In algebra, the missing number to solve for in an equation.

Veritas vos liberabit: Latin phrase; The truth shall set you free.

Vertigo: a dizzying sensation of tilting within stable surroundings or of being in tilting or spinning surroundings.

Voluminous: Of ample size, extent or fullness.

Woodwinds: Instruments in which the sound-generated medium is an enclosed column of air, namely the flute, clarinet, oboe, and saxophone.

Zeus: the supreme ruler of the ancient Greeks, a son of Cronus and Rhea, brother of Demeter, Hades, Hera, Hestia, and Poseidon, and father of a number of rulers and mortals.

Look for these titles from the

Livingstone Library!

Other Titles from Injoy, Inc.

www.injoyinc.com

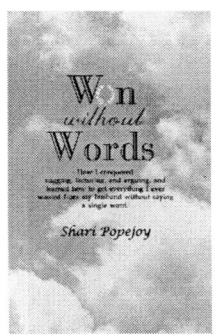

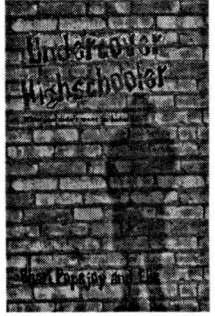